A Little Potato and Hard to Peel

MASCOT
B O O K S
an imprint of Amplify Publishing Group

www.amplifypublishinggroup.com

A Little Potato and Hard to Peel

For more information, please contact:
Mascot Books, an imprint of Amplify Publishing Group
620 Herndon Parkway, Suite 220
Herndon, VA 20170
info@amplifypublishing.com

Library of Congress Control Number: 2023909250

CPSIA Code: PRV1024A

ISBN-13: 978-1-64543-405-4

Printed in the United States

To Pop Pop and my parents

A LITTLE
POTATO
AND HARD TO PEEL

David Harrell

MASCOT
BOOKS
an imprint of Amplify Publishing Group

CHAPTER 1

THE NUB

THE NUB IS WHAT I CALL MY RIGHT HAND. I was born without it. I know that sounds weird, and I guess it looks a little weird too. It's kind of like my hand stopped growing just past my wrist. I have fingers, but they don't look like the fingers you have. They look a little like little dots. Five little dots on top of my wrist. Oh, it doesn't hurt. Just in case you were wondering. It feels like a hand, I guess. It feels like the bottom of the palm of your hand. I can feel things on the nub, and I think it is pretty strong.

When I was a little kid, I wanted to know which was stronger: my hand or my nub. So, I would sit my little brother, Kenneth, down in front of me and ask, "Which is stronger, the hand?" *Punch.* I'd punch him in the arm with my hand. "Or the nub?" *Punch.* I'd punch him in the arm with my nub.

"Owwwwwww!" he'd scream. Then he would get this confused look on his face. "I don't remember. Do it again."

"OK," I'd say. *Punch* with the hand. "The hand?" *Punch* with the nub. "Or the nub?"

1

He would rub his arm and think about it for a few seconds and then say, "The nub!"

We are older now, and he wised up I guess; he doesn't let me hit his arm anymore. Or if I do, he tells Mom, and then I'm in trouble, so it is just not worth it. Well, most of the time it's not worth it. He is a little brother and irritating, so there are definitely times the nub is needed. Maybe not to see if it is stronger, but it is still awesome as a tickling machine.

"Stop it!" he yells through his laughter as I drive the nub into his rib cage.

"Say it," I counter. "Say, 'I love the nub.'" I keep tickling him.

"Boys!" snaps my aunt Carol. "We do not fight in the car. Is your seat belt on, David?"

"Yes, ma'am, it's on," I say. "We are not fighting; I'm just tickling him."

"I don't like it," Kenneth says. "I just want to listen to my music."

"Fine," I say. I put my earphones back on and turn up the volume. We are on a long road trip. It's a family reunion all the way in Kentucky. My grandfather and grandmother are from a small town called Ludlow, Kentucky.

We came to a reunion here a long time ago, so long I don't remember. I was just a baby, and everybody loved passing me around to hug and kiss. We went across the Ohio River to Cincinnati to watch a Cincinnati

Reds baseball game. My parents and grandparents are big baseball fans, by the way. There was this guy who played for the Reds back then; his name was Pete Rose. His nickname was Charlie Hustle. My parents took me to a restaurant or shopping center, and Pete Rose was there signing autographs. My parents brought me up with them for the autograph. Pete Rose looked and me and my hand. "What happened?" he asked. My parents told him I was born without it. "Whoa," he replied. "Well, little fella . . . you just keep hustling." He put out his hand, and I gave him a high five with my nub. He laughed, and my parents took the autograph. I got a Charlie Hustle T-shirt, and once I began to run, my father would take me out to the old baseball field in my neighborhood. He'd sit on the bleachers and watch as I ran the bases in my Charlie Hustle shirt, sliding headfirst into every single one.

Baseball has always been a part of my life. Literally, since the first day. My dad brought a baseball glove to the hospital the day I was born. The story goes, my mom told my dad, "I'm about to have me a baby!"

"You mean a *right now* kinda baby?" questioned my dad.

"Yes! A *right now* kind of baby!"

My dad gently guided my mom down the stairs of their trailer. (Yes, we lived in a trailer the day I was born.) He got her to the beat-up station wagon and said, "Crap, I forgot the glove." He ran back into the trailer, and my mom was just about to pull her hair out. He came back.

"I got it," he said.

"Good . . ." My mom seethed and rolled her eyes.

They got to the hospital, and my mom was taken to her room. She stayed there in labor for twenty-five hours. She was not happy. Funny thing, it was Labor Day Weekend. Finally, on Labor Day, it was go time. They took my mom to the delivery room. My dad stayed in the waiting room. A bunch of my family had come to town. Both sets of grandparents, Pop Pop, Grandma, Poppy and Me Me, my aunts and uncles. It was a pretty big crowd. My dad was nervous but excited. He had that baseball glove. "My kid is going to be a baseball player," he told them. "They are going to be better than I ever was. They're going to be the next great right-handed pitcher, like Goose Gossage!"

The doctor came out with a bit of a concerned gaze. "Everyone is doing fine. Mother is great, and you have a beautiful baby boy." He stopped and took a deep breath before he continued. "Your son is healthy, but there is a slight issue . . . He was born missing his right hand. We don't know why. It could be some of the morning sickness drugs if your wife took those, it could be your exposure to Agent Orange in Vietnam, it could be a combination, or it could be something entirely different. The only thing we know for sure is we don't know why this happened."

I've always imagined time freezing for my dad in that moment. He did go to the war in Vietnam. He survived situations that most of us will never know or experience, but in that moment, time froze. He didn't know what to do. He looked down at this baseball glove in his hand and thought, "How is my son going to play baseball?" He looked up and saw all the faces of the family who were gathered. They all had blank stares. No one had ever heard of someone born without their hand.

My dad put down the baseball glove in a chair in the waiting room. The lump in his chest was growing. He could feel the tears coming into his eyes. He quickly excused himself and went into the bathroom. I'm not sure how long he stayed in there. My uncle always says he went there and collected himself. At some point he came out of the bathroom, and the first thing he did was find that baseball glove he'd put in the chair. He picked up the glove, walked to the family, and said, "My son is just going to play baseball . . . left-handed." With that he joined the doctor and headed into the delivery area to meet me for the first time.

My dad was the first to meet me. My mom was in what they call twilight sleep. Basically, she was knocked out during the birth, so she didn't know yet. Once my mom was awake and alert, they brought me to meet her. My dad was with the doctor and nurses as they brought me in. They told my mom the story. They showed her how beautiful I was. They told her everything else was normal and healthy; it was just this "glitch." My right hand had stopped growing. The doctors and nurses left my parents to themselves. My mom held me, and she cried. She cried a lot. My dad maneuvered his way around her hospital bed to sit next to her and hold her.

"How is he going to tie his shoes?" cried my mom.

"I don't know," said my dad.

"How is he going to ride a bike? Will he go to his prom? Will someone love him? How is he going to climb a tree? How is he going to be a little boy?" My mom started crying so much she couldn't talk anymore.

"I don't know right now," said my dad, "but I can promise you this: we are going to love him, and we are never going to treat him different. He is never going to be different."

My mom looked at me through her wet eyes and smiled. "That's right," she said as she kissed my head. "That's right."

No one in my family had seen anyone who looked like me. They had no idea what to do. My parents came home to find a group of people from their church waiting on the front steps of the trailer. They had covered dishes, desserts, and lots of hugs. One gentleman sat near my mom as she held me. "Have you heard of the Shriners Hospitals?" he asked.

"No," my mom replied.

"Well, they handle these kinds of things. They help children like David. Let me see if I can get you more information."

He did more than that. In a few weeks he called my mom to tell her he had arranged an appointment at the

Shriners Hospital in Jacksonville, Florida. So, when I was six weeks old, we all made our first trip to the Shriners. You may have seen Shriners around. They wear these funny looking fez hats. Anyway, their hospitals are pretty great. They provide health care for children with disabilities or who are burn survivors for very little cost.

When my parents brought me into the Shriners, the first thing they saw was a little girl with no arms and no legs pushing herself through the waiting room on a skateboard. They looked at each other, squeezed hands, and whispered, "We've got this."

I don't remember much of those early visits, obviously. But I do know the Shriners fitted me with my first prosthesis very early. The first prosthesis I got was called the mitt. Oh, right—I should tell you what a prosthesis is. Well, a prosthesis is an artificial arm. Or it could be an artificial leg, but in my case it was an arm, and it looked like a giant winter mitten. It was designed to help someone who was born like me maintain a proper sense of balance. The problem . . . was it was very heavy. So, I learned to crawl with the mitt, and eventually I learned to walk. Although it was a little bit lopsided. It was hard for me to lift the mitt up quickly. My dad's friend Bubba Dubose thought this was very funny. He would hold his hand out and say, "Give me a five, little buddy. Give me a five."

I would try to swing the mitt around to give him a five, and he would move his hand out of the way just in time.

"Ha, ha, ha. You missed!" he would tease. "Come on, let's do it again. Give me a five! Give me a five."

Whoosh. I'd miss again.

"Ha, ha. You see that, Dave? Your boy's just missing."

"Be careful, Bubba. That thing is heavy," my dad warned once.

"Ah, it ain't nothing. Come on, buddy, here you go. Give me a five. Give me a five . . ."

Whack. This time I didn't miss.

"Owwwwwwww! He broke my finger, Dave; he broke my finger. Sweet Jesus, Mary, and Joseph, he broke my finger. Have you got a cold Bud Light I can put on my finger?"

My dad had told him it was heavy.

CHAPTER 2

CAPTAIN HOOK

I WENT TO THE SHRINERS HOSPITAL TWICE A YEAR. Most of the time it was with my dad. I loved the trips. We started going to the hospital in Greenville, South Carolina. It was a little further, but my parents liked it better. We usually stayed the night at Pop Pop and Grandma's. I loved those nights at their house on Pund Avenue. It would be a quick trip, but having one of Grandma's home-cooked meals and singing with them at the piano made just one evening seem like heaven. We'd get up early the next day and drive to a McDonald's just outside of Greenville. I'd get hotcakes, and it was like a king's breakfast. Normally my breakfast was Golden Grahams and milk, but on these days, it was hotcakes with extra syrup.

We would get to the Shriners and have to wait for what seemed like forever in the main waiting area. I would play with other kids. I don't remember anyone specifically. Maybe there were kids who looked like me. I know there were kids missing legs, some used wheelchairs, and some scooted on their bellies or backsides. The one thing we all did have in common was we were kids. We played games like Candy Land, and we solved puzzles of Mickey Mouse. Sometimes we played with action figures: *Star Wars* or G.I. Joe. Sometimes we played with Care Bears. Yuck. We would play until they called our names. Nobody liked this part. When your name was called, you and your family would enter another, smaller waiting room. You could still play a little with the other kids, but it was much quieter in this waiting room. The waiting wasn't as long in this room. They called your name again, and this time you entered a room full of doctors. You were led to a chair in the center of the room. In my case, someone would read from my chart and someone else would hold up my arm so everyone could see. My arm would just hang in the air as a man in a white coat twisted, turned, and bent my arm using words I could not understand.

"Good morning, doctors," the main doctor would begin. "This young patient has a congenital malformation of his right hand. We are not sure if this is caused by fibrous bands of the amnion rupturing in the mother. It is possible these could entangle the fetus and strangle the right limb. It could be teratogenic drugs in the mother or possible exposure to Agent Orange from the father's tour in Vietnam. There is no conclusive evidence. It's just a glitch."

The other doctors would then get up and come to examine my hand, turning and twisting and bending it as they gazed in quizzical fascination. After the doctors took their turns, the main doctor would rub my head and say, "So, young man, how are you doing?"

"I'm doing pretty good," I said once. "I learned a new song. You want to hear it?'

"Sure," the doctor replied.

I'd look around the room at the room full of doctors. I felt my right arm up in the air, my nub held by the doctor standing next to me. I don't know why this song came to mind, but it seemed like I just couldn't help myself. I started to sing.

"*The devil went down to Georgia. He was looking for a soul to steal.*

"*He was in a bind 'cause he was way behind and was looking to make a deal.*"

I grabbed my nub from the doctor and pulled it toward me as if it were a microphone.

"*Fire on the mountain! Run, boys, run. Devil's in the house of the rising sun.*

"*Chicken in the bread pan peckin' out dough. Granny, does your dog bite? No, child, no.*"

I finished with my nub playing a guitar solo, and the doctors stared at me in disbelief. My dad whispered from the back of the room, "Oh, my God."

The doctors clapped and laughed, and the main doctor patted me on the back. "Good to see you, son. Keep up that singing, you hear?"

We were led out and down the lime green–painted hallways to the basement of the Shriners Hospital. It was in the basement that you got to see Bruce. This was my favorite part. Bruce was a prosthetist; he was the one who measured and made my new prostheses. Also, he was a giant. I looked up at him, and he looked down at me. Bruce had an artificial leg . . . and sometimes he let me karate chop it! With my nub!

I took a seat in a chair, and Bruce used a stool on wheels to move from his materials to me and then back again. He had a giant bucket of water, and then he took this casting stuff out. It looked like an ACE bandage but had a chalky consistency. He dropped it in the water, and once it was wet, he began to wrap my arm. I felt the heat of it as it became solid. It was the making of a new prosthesis. Bruce always chats with me. I remember when I was really young, he asked me, "So, David, I hear you are about to start preschool. You know what you want to be when you grow up?"

"A baseball player or a football player," I replied. "I do know I want one of those letterman jackets."

"How do you know what a letterman jacket is?"

"Well, my dad takes me to see the Glynn Academy football team play football on Friday nights, and after the games all the guys come out with their jackets with the big letter on them . . . and they all have girlfriends! I want to be just like them!"

"Well, those are good things to want to be, but you are going to need lots of perseverance."

With that Bruce placed a metal hook on top of the new

prosthesis. Yep, a metal hook stood in for my right hand. It had a strap that went across my back and wrapped around my left shoulder. I would flex my shoulder back to open the hook and flex it forward to close it. It was pretty cool. I could pick things up, and I worked with therapists at the Shriners to learn to tie my shoes.

I was still learning how to use my first metal hook when I went to preschool. I really did want to be a baseball or football player. My dad did take me to football games at old Lanier Field or baseball games at Edo Miller Park. I would dream of the day when I'd come out from the tunnel at Lanier Field and run through the banner the cheerleaders were holding up. I'd dream about my name being called over the PA system at Edo Miller Park. Wearing metal spikes. Oh, and having that letterman jacket. Seeing guys like David Drury, Kevin Yarbrough, Randy Holliman, and Trey Browning after the games or around town in their jackets, the jackets just seemed to radiate like the sun. I want one someday. And a girlfriend. Yeah, if I had those two things, I would be just like everybody else. I'd be normal. Not the guy who wears a hook.

I don't think I thought about the hook too much before preschool. On the first day I went to preschool, I was in a race with a kid, Cliff Tankersley, to be first in line for the glorious slide at the playground. I won the race.

"Hey, Captain Hook," Cliff Tankersley said. "You better watch out with that thing on your arm. You might break somebody's face."

I could feel my heart starting to beat faster.

"Hey, Captain Hook, you ever find that alligator, Captain Hook? You might find it in your mama's bathtub. Captain Hook! Captain Hook! Captain Hook!"

"Rrrrrrrrrrrrrrrrr!" I screamed as I lifted up my hook at Cliff Tankersley and swung.

I missed. He took off running, and I chased him all the way back to the school building. Then I ran back to the slide because now I was going to be the first in line. I climbed up the ladder, I reached out my arm . . . and for the first time I saw it, I mean really *saw* it: my hook. I looked down at all the other kids looking up at me, and I realized my parents had lied to me when I was born. I was different.

I just stood at the top of the slide for what seemed like forever. I didn't want to slide anymore. The rest of the day seems a blur to me. I do remember that Cliff Tankersley's mama was waiting for my mama at the end of preschool that day. "You need to tell your son to stay away from my Cliffy with that *thing* he's got on his arm."

"Well, you need to tell your son to stop calling other kids names." My mom put her arm around me to pull me close as we turned to walk to our car. "You big heifer!" she whispered over her shoulder. When we got to the car and started to drive away, my mom said, "David, you have to wear your hook, and you have to be careful with your right hand." I could see my mom biting her lip. I knew she wanted to cry, but she didn't. She just nodded and focused on the road ahead.

That night the preschool director called my parents. "Hello, Mr. and Mrs. Harrell. I am very concerned about the incident we had on our playground today. The *thing* David is wearing on his arm is very dangerous, and we cannot have him terrorizing other kids on the playground. Other parents are expressing concerns, and after much thought, I think it is best for David not to come back to our school."

My parents put down the phone. My mom was fuming. "You need to go warm up the station wagon. If that lady wants to see terrorizing, I will drive over there right now and show her how we take care of things . . . South Georgia–style."

"Honey, let's just calm down a little," my dad replied. "Can I get you a Bud Light?"

My mom calmed down, and the next day she called the only other preschool in my town. It was Ms. Tina's Playhouse. Ms. Tina was a little eccentric for South Georgia. I think that was why my mom was hesitant about bringing me there. We walked into Ms. Tina's school, and the first thing she did was go down to one knee, look me in the eye, and take my left hand in hers, then take my metal hook in her other. She sang in her raspy voice:

"*You are a promise. You are a possibility.*

You are a promise with a capital P.

Come here, you little sugar puss." She brought me

into her arms for one of the tightest hugs I'd ever gotten. She kept holding my hand as she led me through the classroom and introduced me to the other kids. "This is David, everyone. He is a wonder, just like each one of you."

I loved Ms. Tina's Playhouse. It felt like home. The kids treated me like I was just one of the other kids. One day Ms. Tina said to me, "David, you are a little performer, aren't you? I think you would be wonderful as the third Billy Goat Gruff!"

I *loved* playing the third Billy Goat Gruff. I remember performing for the other parents, having their eyes on me, and making them laugh. "I'm climbing the great big mountain to eat the lush spring grass!" I'd say with my papier mâché antlers. It felt good to be included.

I think I was lucky my mom found her way to Ms. Tina's. I didn't know it at the time, but I left there with confidence. I didn't really think about my hook much. I haven't thought about it much, but lately I'm starting to notice it more. I'm starting middle school this fall, and not just middle school but a new school with new kids. My mom is switching me to a middle school that is in a different zone than the one I'm supposed to go to. She is moving to teach at a new elementary school and wants my little brothers to come to that school with her. That school is zoned for this new middle school, so I will go there with very few friends. I'm not looking forward to it.

CHAPTER 3

POP POP AND THE LITTLE POTATOES

"HERE WE ARE," says my aunt Carol.

We arrive at the hotel for the family reunion. The best part is there is a pool. I play with my brothers and my cousins all day until it's time to get dressed and head to the church for the reunion. I want to wear my Charlie Hustle T-shirt, but my mom insists I wear a collared shirt. Boring. We get to the reunion, and it's pretty boring. There are so many people I don't know, and there is no way I'm going to remember everyone my mom is introducing me to. If I hear "you've gotten so big, David" one more time, I'm going to pull my hair out. The food is pretty good, and I like my cousin Johnny. He lives here in Ohio.

"Wanna pop?" he asks me.

"What's a pop?" I reply.

"A soda?" he asks.

"You mean a Coke?" I ask. He nods with a confused look on his face. "Sure," I say, and we head to the kitchen to get a Coke. It's actually a Dr. Pepper, but where I am from, we call everything a Coke.

We come back into the fellowship hall, and I see my granddad, Pop Pop, go up to the microphone.

"Hi, everyone. I hope you are all having a grand evening. I know you all know how much I love to sing and dance; the only thing I love more is my beautiful wife Catherine. So Kitsy, come on up here. Hit it, maestro." My aunt Ruth starts to play a song on the piano, and Pop Pop takes my grandma's hand and begins to dance with her as he sings. He is so smooth in the way he moves. He guides my grandmother effortlessly while he sings.

"*When your hair has turned to silver, I will love you just the same.*

"*I will only call you sweetheart. That will always be your name . . .*"

It is beautiful watching them dance and sing. I can't imagine my grandma without silver hair, but I guess they really were young and in love. Here in this moment they are still in love and still making everyone laugh. I watch them and then watch the crowd. Pop Pop knows how to play to the crowd. He knows all eyes are on him, and he is entertaining us all. For just a second my mind goes back to when I performed in *The Three Billy Goats Gruff* at Ms. Tina's or when I was the little drummer boy for my church's Christmas concert. That feeling of all eyes on me. I smile because I love that feeling too. I smile because I love watching Pop Pop work the room. He finishes the song and playfully dips my grandma to end the dance. Everyone applauds. I look around, and it seems everyone has a tissue and is drying their eyes. I tingle because I know it is beautiful. I know it is real.

The next day we all gather in my aunt's van, and Pop Pop gives us a tour of his hometown, Ludlow, Kentucky. It's just across the river from Cincinnati, Ohio. We stop at the riverfront, and you can see the city of Cincinnati across the water. I have a thought about how far it would be to swim there. Pop Pop comes up next to me and says, "Lots of kids would try to swim over to Cincinnati in the summertime. Not a lot of them made it. There were a lot of boats that had to go and pick up kids in the middle of the river." He pats my shoulder, and we join the others for a walk through the neighborhood.

We walk up and down the sloping hills of Ludlow. Pop Pop tells stories of friends and adventures he had on certain streets. It's good to hear his stories. He is a great storyteller. We come up this one street, and Pop Pop says, "Hmmmm, this was our street." He gets a little sad. He kind of slows down his pace of walking like he isn't sure if he wants to keep going. But he does. "Yep, this one up here. This was our house," he says.

It's a beautiful townhouse. "It sure wasn't this nice when we were here," Pop Pop says with a laugh. His father died when he was very young. His older brother quit school and went to work to help support the family, but then he died soon after. His mother made the house into a bed-and-breakfast, and Pop Pop worked to keep the guests happy and the house in good repair.

We are all standing in front of the house listening to Pop Pop tell us stories about the house when a lady opens the front door. "Hello," she says. "Can I help you with anything?"

"We're sorry," my mom replies. "This is my daddy, and he grew up in this house. He hasn't been back in so long; we were just reminiscing. Sorry to bother you."

"You're not bothering me at all. Would you like to come in and see the inside?" she says as she opens the screen door.

"That would be amazing," my mom replies and takes my granddad's hand to help him up to the front porch.

As Pop Pop walks up the stairs and into the house, it seems like there is this force that hits him. Not like the Force in *Star Wars* but this weight. Maybe it's all the memories coming back. He talks about how the house looked when he lived there and how it's different but so much is the same. He puts his hand on the banister of the staircase and just looks at it for a long time. Then he slowly goes up the stairs, his hand bringing along memories as he holds on and glides up the banister.

We explore the house and drink fresh lemonade from the owner. She is so nice to let us come and walk around her house. It means a lot to Pop Pop; I can tell. On our way back to our van, I see an old baseball field. It's a block or so away. "Mom, can we go by that old ball field?" I ask. I still like going to ball fields and running the bases.

"Noooooo!" cries my little brother Kenneth. "I just want to go back to the hotel. I'm hungry!"

"We should get back, David," my mom says. "It's getting close to lunchtime, and there is a pool at the hotel."

"You know, I'd like to see that old baseball field too," says Pop Pop. "Kathy, I can take David while you take the others back. Just come back and pick us up after you get them settled with lunch."

My mom looks at me and knows immediately this is what I want to do. "OK," she says. "You guys have fun, and I'll be back in a few."

"Wait," I say as I run to the trunk of the van. I grab my baseball glove prosthesis and Kenneth's glove for Pop Pop. "Is it cool if Pop Pop uses your glove, Kenneth?"

"Sure. Whatever," he replies.

"Come on, Pop Pop. I've got you a glove so we can play catch." Pop Pop laughs and joins me walking up the block to the old baseball field.

The Shriners made me a glove attachment to put onto my prosthesis. I take the hook off and attach the glove. It works the same way my hook works. There is a figure-eight strap that goes over my left shoulder, and when I flex my shoulder back, it opens, and flexing it forward closes it. I've been playing baseball for a while now and have been using this glove prosthesis since farm league.

My farm league team was called the Coca-Cola Reds. I remember coming to practice the first day. My coach was

Mr. Bullock. We worked on fielding ground balls. "Get your tailgates down, boys!" Coach Bullock would say. He was a great coach and really helped me learn to field the ball with my prosthetic glove. I played all over the field, but my favorite position was catcher. I loved wearing the leg guards, the chest protector, and the mask. The smell of the leather around the face guard of the mask was awesome. In farm league, the coaches pitched to you, so I didn't have to use a catcher's mitt. It was mostly just fielding ground balls if the batter missed the pitch. I could keep my tailgate down.

One game, it was the bottom of the last inning and we were winning. The tying run was on second, and the batter hit a ball toward left field. Our best player, Brandon Highsmith, was playing shortstop. He fielded the ball, and the runner on second rounded third, trying to score. Brian threw the ball to home plate. It bounced right in front of me, and I caught it on the short hop and dove to tag the runner with my prosthetic glove. "You're out!" said the umpire as I rolled through the clay dirt and showed the ball in my glove.

The whole team ran toward me and celebrated! We jumped up and down, hugging each other like we'd just won the National League pennant. "Way to go, Hot Dog!" Coach Bullock said. "You are high-quality, top-grade American hot dog, David!" I'm not sure why Coach Bullock called me "Hot Dog", but I liked it. It made me feel special.

My mom and dad were cheering from the stands too. It was a great moment. Our team, the Coca-Cola Reds, won first place that year. We got a big trophy. I love that trophy. It makes me remember I am special; I am good at something. I was one of the better players on our team. It feels good to be good at something.

"Here you go, catch," says Pop Pop as he throws me the ball. We've gotten to the old baseball field. It is definitely old. It's seen better days, but you can feel there is history here. It has been a part of this town for a long time. I catch the ball and throw it back to Pop Pop. He pretends to tag someone out and makes cheering noises. I laugh. Pop Pop always makes me laugh. "So, David. You're about to start middle school, right? You think you know what you want to be when you grow up?"

"I don't know," I say as I catch his next throw. "A baseball player," I say with smile. "I do know that I want a letterman jacket."

"A letterman jacket? Why is that so important?" he asks.

"Well, my dad takes me to see the Glynn Academy high school football games and baseball games. And when I see those guys in town, they all have those letterman jackets . . . and they all have girlfriends. I don't know. I just want to be just like them," I say.

Pop Pop laughs.

"Bruce at the Shriners Hospital once told me I would need lots of perseverance. I'm not sure if I know what that means."

Pop Pop nods his head and grins. "You know what, David? Perseverance is a lot like my Little League baseball team. We played on this very field. We were called the Little Potatoes and Hard to Peel."

"That's a funny name." I laugh.

"Well, we were smaller than the other kids and maybe not as talented, but we always played with our hearts. So, it didn't matter if we won or lost. We never got down, because we knew on the inside . . . we were tough and hard to peel."

Pop Pop winks at me and pretends to tag another imaginary base runner. I laugh, and we continue to play catch until my mom comes back to pick us up. I watch that old ball field from the window of the car as we leave. I imagine Pop Pop as a kid in this pin-striped baseball uniform with "Little Potatoes and Hard to Peel" on the front. I guess he is serious, but what a funny name for a baseball team!

We get back to the hotel, and there is just enough time for me to join my brothers and cousins in the pool. We swim and play and enjoy the summer sunset. It is as close to a perfect day as you can get.

CHAPTER 4

MR. MO

THE NEXT MORNING there is a strange feeling in the hotel. My mom and aunt Carol are gone. My great aunt Mary is there with us at the hotel. She says my grandma was taken to the hospital last night and that my mom and aunt Carol have been there all night.

"There's nothing to worry about right now," she tells me and my older cousin Dena. "Your grandma was just feeling ill, and they want to make sure she is OK. It is really just being overly precautious."

"OK," I reply.

"You just need to be strong for your little brothers and cousins, OK?"

"Yes, ma'am," we say in unison.

We get our breakfast together, and aunt Mary helps get breakfast for the younger ones. My mom calls and tells us that we are going to have to leave early and aunt Mary is going to drive us to her house in Atlanta and my dad will pick us up there. "You need to get home and ready for the All-Star tryouts," she tells me.

"Is Grandma all right?" I ask.

"We think so, sweetheart. She is just having a little trouble with her heart, and the doctor wants to be careful. They are going to keep her here for a couple of days and make sure she is better. Pop Pop is here with her, so she is in good hands. He is singing to her and keeping her happy."

I knew Pop Pop would be there, and it's not a surprise at all that he is singing to her. He always says he wanted to be a song and dance man but never got the chance. He had to go to work when he was still so young. He never really got to dream. "Dream," I think. Right, my dream of being a baseball player, of getting that letterman jacket. My mom was right. I have All-Star tryouts for baseball next week. All of a sudden all I want is to get home and practice.

The trip with aunt Mary is fine. It is nice getting to know her. She married my grandma's younger brother Jim. We talk about stories of times they spent time with Pop Pop and Grandma. I love listening to her stories about the fun adventures they had traveling or just visiting and singing together. The trip to Atlanta isn't too long, and my dad arrives the next morning. We get into my dad's car and head for home.

I jump right into baseball when I get home. The All-Star tryouts are coming up, and I need to get better if I want to make the All-Star team. I mean, I've got to make that team. I've always been one of the better players, but this year has been more challenging.

I am having trouble using my prosthetic glove to catch the ball. The ball is coming to me faster, I guess. The big problem for me is I'm having trouble turning the glove to catch a ball over my head. I used to be able to keep the glove near my chest and catch the ball like a basket, but now that is getting harder and harder to do. I started this year at second base, and most of the time I have to catch ground balls, which is easy, but it's been hard to catch balls from the third baseman or shortstop to turn a double play. Now that I am in the junior league, that is happening more often. It's really just a couple levels from high school. So, in midseason this year, Coach Bullock moved me to right field.

That is the last place you want to be. It's usually where you put someone who is terrible! Am I terrible? In the last game I played before the reunion, I was in right field. We were winning by a run in the last inning, and there were two outs! A guy hit a fly ball out to me in right field. It was high, but it's a ball I almost always catch. I saw it coming, and I ran to get under it. I began to realize it was going further than I thought, and I couldn't get the prosthetic glove to move over my head. The ball fell to the ground and rolled all the way to the fence. I heard the other team's fans start cheering. I saw Jason Bronson, our center fielder, running with me to the fence. I went to the ball, picked it up, and threw it as hard as I could to the cutoff man. It was too late; the guy made it all the way home with the winning run. I threw the ball so hard

I fell on the ground. I lay there in the outfield grass by myself listening to the other team celebrate. How could I be so bad at something I used to be so good at?

I go to the All-Star tryouts and am put into right field. I try to be positive, but I miss two fly balls. I even miss a ground ball; I never do that. I am so frustrated.

The list of All-Stars comes out, and I am not on the list.

"Sorry, Hot Dog," says Coach Bullock. "I tried to put in a good word for you, but the other coaches just don't think you've got the tools this year. Keep your head up and keep working to get better. You'll have your name on this list next year . . . OK, Hot Dog?"

He gives me a hug as he sees the tears well up in my eyes. My dad finds me and realizes immediately what has happened. He comes over and rubs my head.

"Let's get out of here, bud." I go to my dad's car and slump in the back seat. I just want to be alone. I stare at my prosthetic glove and hook. It's their fault I can't play as fast as I want to play. I think about my missing right hand. That is the problem. If I was born with two hands, I'd never have to use these stupid prosthetics anyway.

I see my dad looking at me from the rearview mirror. We park the car in the driveway, and my dad asks, "You all right, bud?"

"No," I reply.

"I know it hurts pretty good to not make that team, but sometimes life doesn't work out just the way we want it to."

"Yeah, like not having a stupid hand, I guess." I throw my hook and glove to the ground.

"Don't do that, son. Your hand has nothing to do with this."

"Really, Dad? I think it has everything to do with it. If I had two hands, I wouldn't have to wear this stupid prosthesis, and I would be able to catch the ball and play just as fast as everybody else. It's not fair!"

"Well, life isn't fair."

"I didn't ask for this, Dad!" I scream, putting my missing right hand in the air. "And if you hadn't come back from Vietnam with that Agent Orange all over you, none of this would have happened! It's your fault I am like this, and it's your fault my name's not on that list!"

I open the door, run from the car, and go straight to my room. I throw my glove and hook in my closet. I punch the wall with my nub. It doesn't stop the anger; it just puts a small hole in the drywall. I feel this swelling inside me, like I'm about to explode. I hit the pillow on my bed. That feels better than the wall. I hit it and hit it until I see the trophy from the Coca-Cola Reds. It's gold ballplayer swinging the bat on top of a golden baseball. I look at it with the memory of catching the ball from Brandon Highsmith coming back in my mind. The team celebrating with me. It was all a lie. I am not good at baseball. I can never be with this hand. I am a loser, and I don't deserve this trophy.

I storm downstairs and get a trash bag from the

kitchen. I shove the trophy into the trash bag and start to put anything I've accomplished in the bag. Certificates from school, cards from my grandparents, trophies from other sports, my archery trophy from Cub Scouts. All of it is a lie. I will never be anything because of this . . . mistake. The universe failed me.

I take the trash bag downstairs and go through the garage to get to the trash can. As I get to the end of the garage, I hear something. It is sobbing. My dad. My dad is sobbing, leaning against the trunk of his car. He doesn't see me. I hide near the wall of the garage. I've never seen my dad cry; my dad doesn't cry; I made my dad cry. All of my anger evaporates and turns to guilt. What have I done?

I carry the trash bag back inside and quickly go back to my room; my eyes are full of tears. It starts slowly but turns into a full-blown ugly cry. The anger comes back, but it's anger at what I said to my dad. I stare at my nub.

"It's OK, you fool," says my nub.

Yes. My nub talks. I know it is strange, but ever since I was a little kid, I've pretended my nub talks. I've always thought the fingers on my nub look like a mohawk, and I pretend that there are a couple of eyes, and my thumb becomes the nose. I think he looks like a British punk rocker, and I call him Mr. Mo.

"I said it's OK, fool," Mr. Mo says in my mind.

"No, it's not, Mr. Mo. I went too far. I don't know why I said it. It's not his fault. It's nobody's fault. I just . . ."

"You just got upset, fool. It happens. Do you believe it? Do you believe you can only be a loser?" he asks.

I look at the trash bag full of my stuff. It looks so silly. I feel so silly.

"I don't know, Mr. Mo. I feel like I am not as good as the other kids now. I know I'm not as good as the other kids now. I can see them playing faster now. I want to play faster too, but I don't know how."

"I know how you can play faster," Mr. Mo says.

"How?" I question suspiciously.

"Take off the prosthesis. Put a glove on your left hand."

"That is not going to work," I reply.

"Just get a glove and let me show you," Mr. Mo says firmly.

I go to the hall closet and find my brother's glove. He uses it on his left hand. I go back to my room and shut the door.

"Now put the glove on your left hand. You will catch the ball, roll it over on me, then take the ball and throw it with your left hand. Give it a try," says Mr. Mo.

I put the glove on my left hand, I pretend to catch the ball, and I start to roll it onto my right arm. I use my nub to help roll the glove over. The imaginary ball rolls into my left hand, and I throw the ball in my mind. I try it again. I try it again but faster. I keep doing it faster and faster. "This could work!" I say. I feel the excitement growing. I can get faster and better at baseball. There is a sudden drop in my stomach. I remember my dad. What

I said to him. The image of him sobbing.

"You gotta take care of that, fool," says Mr. Mo. I know he is right.

I walk back toward the garage. My dad is in the kitchen putting away dishes.

"Hey, Dad," I say hesitantly.

"Hey, bud," he replies as he keeps working.

"I'm really sorry for what I said. I . . . I . . ."

"It's OK, bud. I know you were upset, and I know you really wanted to make that All-Star team."

"But it's not OK, Dad. It's not your fault I was born like this. I don't know why I said that . . ." I start to tear up.

"Hey, son. It's OK. I love you," my dad says as he brings me in for a hug.

I cry into his shoulder. He just holds me and lets me get it all out. "Listen," he finally says. "We are going to keep practicing and keep working on baseball. We will get better, I promise."

I wipe my eyes and say, "I think I have an idea how I can get better." I run to get my brother's glove. "What if I put the glove on my left hand and catch it? I can then roll the glove on my right arm, take the ball, and throw it."

"Let's give it a try," my dad says. He grabs a baseball from the garage, brings it in the kitchen, and gives me a nod. He tosses the ball underhand toward me. I catch it with my left hand and roll the glove onto my right hand. It's a little awkward, but I get the ball and toss it back. My dad looks at me and nods slowly. "It will take some practice, but this just might work."

"I'm really going to need your help, Dad," I say.

"I tell you what: we will throw outside every day, and if you can catch then throw the ball and get the glove back on before I throw it back to you, I'll let you play with the glove on your left hand."

I nod. "It's a deal," I say.

My dad keeps his part of the deal. We throw almost every day after he gets home from work the next week. I also throw the ball against the side of the house when he is not there. I keep practicing and practicing, and pretty soon I am just about as fast as someone with two hands.

On Sunday afternoon I'm throwing the ball against the wall of the house after church. My dad comes out and says, "David, come over here. I've got something to show you."

It's a newspaper article from *USA Today*. There's a picture of a guy with a USA baseball hat on, and his right arm looks just like mine.

"This guy is Jim Abbott," my dad says. "He was born just like you, and he is going to pitch for the USA in the Pan-American games. It seems like he is playing the same way you are trying to do. Looks like your idea is definitely going to work."

I read the article. It's true. Jim Abbott taught himself to play baseball with the glove on his left hand. He rolls the glove onto his nub just like Mr. Mo taught me. Not only is he pitching for the USA, but he is pitching for the University of Michigan. He is a real baseball player. What I am doing is right. The way I am adapting is going to make me better. I am going to be good at baseball. I lift my arms into the air, victorious, the newspaper in my left and my baseball glove on my right. Then I have a new thought . . . I start middle school tomorrow.

CHAPTER 5

LIL' ABNER

"**ABNER HARRELL.**" Mrs. Harper looks up above her glasses. "Abner Harrell." She sits up, looking around the classroom above her glasses as they stay firmly on her nose. "Abner Harrell?" she asks more forcefully.

"Here," I reluctantly reply, raising my left hand slightly.

"Ha! Abner." A kid laughs as he points in my direction. "Lil Abner! Ha, ha, ha." The other kids in class laugh along with him.

"Excuse me, Christopher Lancaster," Mrs. Harper sharply says, looking again from above her glasses. Everyone is silent immediately, but the damage is done.

Abner David Harrell III is my full name. I am named after my father, Abner David Harrell, Jr., and his dad is Abner David Harrell, Sr. Actually, the name Abner Harrell dates back to 1782 when Abner Harrell made his way from North Carolina to southern Georgia. It's not a direct line of names from 1782, but it is kinda cool to share something with my dad and my granddad. But Abner? It's not an easy name to have in middle school.

I rush out of Mrs. Harper's class as soon as the bell rings. "See ya later, Lil Abner," Christopher Lancaster sneers as I pass through the door. I rush to my next class, Mrs. Flowers' math class, so I am first in the class. I come in the door in a hurry.

"Hello, young man. You seem to be on a mission." Mrs. Flowers laughs.

"Yes. Hello. Um, I'm David Harrell, and I have a quick question. On your class roster, I am listed by my first name, Abner. Is there any way you could just call me David? It's my middle name and the one I'd like to use."

"No problem, sweetheart," Mrs. Flowers says with a wink.

The rest of the class starts to arrive, and I go to find my desk. I think I've headed off any more Abner talk for the day. Maybe the other kids will just forget.

Mrs. Flowers calls attendance. "Toby Gibson."

"Here," the kid Toby calls.

"Abner Harrell," Mrs. Flowers says in what feels like the loudest voice in the world.

"Oh, no," I say to myself.

"Oops. I mean, David Harrell," Mrs. Flowers says with a silent "I'm sorry" whisper to me.

"Here," I say, raising my hand.

"Ha! Abner!" comes from the back of the class. The classroom laughs. Christopher Lancaster. Is he going to be in every one of my classes?

The Lil Abner taunts run their course in a week or so.

Teachers finally remember to make a note and call me David. The bigger problem is I don't really know anyone at this school. There are a couple of guys from baseball I know, but we're not good friends. No one from my elementary school is here. It's just a new world.

I start to make a name for myself in PE class. I can throw the football well, and I can catch it using my nub! On an especially good day, I jump up and catch the ball right in front of Christopher Lancaster. He falls in the dirt, and I run all the way for a touchdown. I raise my hands, and my team joins me to celebrate in the end zone.

"Now that's a great catch!" says Coach Ferris, our PE teacher. Everyone seems impressed. Everyone, perhaps, but Christopher Lancaster.

If there is one downside to PE, it's that I get so sweaty. I try to clean off, but it is pretty clear I just gave 100 percent in PE when I come to Ms. Saunders's art class.

"Do we need another paper towel, David?" she asks with a slightly disapproving look.

"Yes, ma'am," I reply and grab a few extra to help dry off.

We are working on a group project in art class. We move to our tables to work together making a collage of things we enjoy about fall. I've drawn a big football and a red-and-white letterman jacket. I really want to be like the guys who wear those jackets in high school. I'm doing my best to cut out the drawings, but like always, there are no lefty scissors in the art cart! Why must left-handed people always get the shaft? I am clearly struggling to cut out my drawings when I hear:

"Do you want some help?"

I look up to see Samantha Parker. I'm sure it's just because she's sitting in front of the window, but I swear there's this angelic glow that surrounds her as I stare just long enough to make it awkward.

"Ummm, yes," I finally stumble to say and hand my football and letterman jacket pictures her way. She smiles and takes the right-handed scissors from me.

"So, you want to be a football player?" she asks.

"Maybe," I reply in my best attempt to be cool.

"Are you going to the game this Friday? I think there are going to be a lot of people there."

"Yeah, I am totally going to be there."

"Good." She smiles.

I smile too. I smell her perfume. Butterflies start a dance party in my stomach. She smells so good. I move just a little closer to her, pretending to be interested in her cutting out my drawings. A drop of sweat falls right on the paper. I am reminded of my sweaty self . . . As good as she smells, I must be the antithesis of it.

"There you go," she says as she hands me back the pictures. "I guess you can handle the glue, right?"

"Totally. I got it." I take the cutouts and apply the glue. I add them to our collage. Samantha adds red, orange, and yellow leaves. She also adds several pumpkins.

The bell rings, and we all gather our stuff. "See you

at the game Friday," I say to Samantha as we walk out of class. All her friends look at me and then at her. Samantha just nods and walks quickly away.

"Smooth move, ace." Dean Sabacan snickers as he walks past. Yeah, that was definitely not a smooth move.

CHAPTER 6

FOOTBALL NIGHT IN GEORGIA AND THE GREAT CAFETERIA KERFUFFLE

BOOM. BOP, BA, BOP, BOP go the drums from the band. You can hear them all the way from the parking lot. "Stay where I can see you!" my mom says loudly. I shrink into my sweatshirt as we walk toward the entrance gate. We can see the lights of the stadium shining down on the field as we get closer. We get to the gate, and my mom takes our tickets from her purse.

"You keep an eye on your brother, OK?" she says as we enter the stadium. "We'll meet at this concession stand at the end of the game. Understand?"

"Yes, ma'am," I reply and walk quickly toward the ramp to the grandstands. I love the way the ramp is dark and the lights grow as you walk up toward the field. The brick wall lines the first rows of the grandstands. I look up to the seats that seem to go on forever toward the sky. The band is playing music, and the cheerleaders are leading the students in chants. The excitement is growing. I see some guys from my classes at school: Dean Sabacan, Wyman Dickerson, and David Kane. I usually just call him Kane. They seem safe. "Let's go. Follow me," I tell my brother.

We climb up the stairs past the high school students, and soon I begin to recognize the middle schoolers. We make our way toward Dean, Wyman, and Kane. "What's up, guys?" I say. They nod a "what's up" back, and we stand on the bleachers.

Soon, the band has made its way onto the field. They create two lines from the huge paper banner saying "Let's Go Glynn Academy." The excitement builds as the football team gathers behind the banner. The band starts to play the school fight song, and the team tears through the banner as they run onto the field. We are jumping and screaming in celebration! A couple of high schoolers hand red-and-white pom-poms to us, and we are all shaking them and cheering as the game gets underway.

"I can't wait until I run out on the field like that!" I say loudly to my brother.

"Yeah, right," I hear somebody say behind me. I look back to see Christopher Lancaster. "You are going to play football? Ha, Lil Abner is going to be a one-handed football player." Everyone around laughs.

"He caught a pass over you in PE," says Wyman.

"Yeah, well, that was without pads and just two-hand touch," Christopher replies defensively. "Oh, and I saw you talking to Samantha Parker the other day, Lil Abner. Ha, ha, ha. You really think you are going to get a girl-friend? Who's going to go out with someone like you?"

The crowd suddenly erupts. I look toward the field, and T.J. Fisher has just caught the opening kickoff and is running away from everyone down the sideline. We all are jumping up and screaming, "Run, T.J., run!" Touchdown! Everyone high fives. Even Christopher Lancaster gives me a high five. The touchdown ends the conversation, and I take the opportunity to bring my brother downstairs for a giant pretzel and soft drinks.

As we come back up the stands, I see Samantha Parker and a bunch of the girls from school sitting a few rows up from the band. I walk up the stairs toward them. "Why are we going this way?" my brother asks.

"Don't worry about it," I quickly reply.

"Our seats are over that way," Kenneth whines.

"Don't worry about it!" I say forcefully.

We walk up past the band. Everyone is still happy from T.J. Fisher's touchdown. The girls are all talking and laughing. Samantha Parker looks at me. She smiles and gives me a wave. I give a nod of my head and just keep walking up. We go three or four rows up and sit in the next section.

"This is the parents' section," Kenneth says.

"Shut up," I say back. "Here, have some popcorn."

We sit and watch the game from the slightly emptier parents' section. I stare down at where the girls are sitting. There are no boys sitting with them. Should I go say hi? It feels like a mistake. So I just sit there with my brother and watch the game. I kinda want to avoid Christopher Lancaster and some of those other guys. Glynn Academy wins twenty-four to seven, and we make our way back to meet my mom and youngest brother at the concession stand.

"Enjoy the game?" my mom asks.

"Sure," I say.

"We sat in the parents' section like weirdos," Kenneth mumbles.

"Why was that?" asks Mom.

"He's too scared to talk to girls." Kenneth laughs.

"No. I just . . . I just wanted to see the game better. All the students were standing, and it was hard to see the field."

"Whatever." Kenneth sighs.

"Well, I'm glad you got to see the game. How about those Glynn Academy Red Terrors?" My mom waves her pom-pom in our faces.

"Yeah!" I laugh.

We get into the minivan and head home. We all get in pj's and get ready for bed. I can't stop thinking about why I didn't say hi to Samantha Parker. I could've just waved. Is that so hard? Or stopped and said hi. "How do you get a girlfriend?" I ask out loud.

"It's a numbers game, fool." I look down to my nub. Mr. Mo is there. "It's really a numbers game, fool."

"What does that mean? The more girls I ask out, the better my chances are?" I ask.

"Well, kinda," he responds.

"So, right. I have an idea. I could ask out all the girls at the girls' table in the lunchroom. What's your prediction, Mr. Mo?"

"Pain."

"Whatever, Mr. Mo," I think. I now have a plan. I now have a mission. I'm going to get a girlfriend, and it is going to happen Monday . . . at lunch.

My heart is racing as I enter the cafeteria. The line seems to be moving slower today. I keep an eye on the girls' table as it begins to fill up. Leslie St. Claire, Julie Fisher, and Heather Bruce are already seated. More will be coming soon. I pick up my tray and get my lunch. It is meat loaf and mashed potatoes.

"One scoop of potatoes or two, sweetie?" asks the lady behind the counter.

"Two, please," I say, not looking, trying to keep my eyes on the girls' table. Betsy Kennedy, Brandy Roundtree, and Samantha Parker are now sitting there too.

I try to take deep breaths as I walk toward their table. I pass my regular table. I see Dean, Wyman, and Kane look at me. That is when everything seems to go in slow motion. I think I hear Dean ask "Where is he going?" with his mouth still full of mashed potatoes. I put my tray down at the girls' table and pull a chair from another table. The surprised looks on the girl's faces are palpable.

"Hi. Um, Leslie," I start. I'm not sure why I choose Leslie—I think because she happens to be right in front of me. "I was wondering if you'd like to be my girlfriend and you know . . . go with me?"

Leslie's eyes look immediately down to her bagged lunch. I think her jaw drops down so far that it also almost touches said bagged lunch.

"No . . ." she says quietly under her breath.

I immediately look to the left. "Julie, hi. I was wondering if you would like to be my girlfriend and you know . . . go with me?"

Julie Fisher's lips rise almost like she's doing an Elvis impersonation or perhaps as though she sees a car crash. The puzzled look on her face made the firmly stated "no" seem to sting a little less.

I look to the end of the table. Samantha. Samantha Parker. "Samantha, I was wondering . . ." I begin to say. Before I can finish, the girls all begin to get up to leave the table. They leave quickly to find another place to sit. Samantha gets up as well. She looks at me and then slowly shakes her head no. She quickly joins the other girls.

I start to feel a lot of eyes on me. Thank goodness for the chaos of the lunchroom. Not everybody saw, but enough did. I quickly take my tray and walk with my head down to my regular table.

"Dude," Dean said. "That was brutal."

"Gutsiest move I ever saw, man," echoes Wyman. "But . . . yeah . . . that was brutal."

Luckily for me there is a tornado drill that afternoon and two eighth graders are caught making out in the music room during the drill. That takes away any attention from my cafeteria kerfuffle.

"I pity the girl who doesn't go with you! A pox upon her house," says Mr. Mo while I'm brushing my teeth in the bathroom that night.

"Not now, Mr. Mo. I was just doing what you told me to do," I replied.

"I didn't tell you to ask out a table full of girls, fool!"

"Well, they don't want to be my girlfriend because I'm not normal. You know that is true. What can I do to be normal enough for them to want to go with me?" I ask.

"Everything going all right in there?" my mom asks as she knocks on the door.

"Um, yes. Everything's OK," I say.

"OK. Well, don't forget we are going to the Shriners Hospital next week, and you need to make sure your teachers send all your assignments to the hospital. You are going to be at the Shriners for a full week. You are going to have that cool new myoelectric hand. Now, hurry up in there. Your brother has to poop."

"There you go, fool," Mr. Mo says. "You go to the

Shriners and come back with two hands."

"Of course," I say silently. "Two hands and I can be normal enough for them to go with me."

CHAPTER 7

IT'S MYOELECTRIC, BOOGIE WOOGIE WOOGIE

I HAVE GONE TO THE SHRINERS HOSPITAL many times in my life, but I've never stayed there overnight. This trip I have to stay a full week in the hospital by myself. I don't think I've ever stayed away from my parents for more than a night. I'm excited but also a little scared. My mom and dad drive me up this time. We stop to spend the night with Pop Pop and Grandma. We leave early in the morning and make the regular stop for hotcakes at the McDonald's on the way. I go to see Bruce like always, and he brings out the myoelectric arm. It looks like a real hand—as much as a prosthesis can look like a real hand. There are two sensors inside the arm. They line up with the muscles in my arm. If I flex my arm upward, the hand opens, and if I flex down, the hand closes.

"Give it a try," Bruce says.

I practice opening and closing the hand. I can hear the motor moving as the hand opens and closes.

"Here," Bruce says. "Grab this pencil from my hand."

I focus on moving the hand close to the pencil and then flex downward with my arm to close the hand around the pencil. I take it from Bruce.

"Great job, David! Now see if you can pick it up from the table." Bruce takes the pencil and moves it to the table.

This time it is much harder to grab the pencil. It takes a couple of times trying to pick it up. I roll the pencil across the table a couple of times before finally gathering it into the fingers of the mechanical hand.

"Wow. That is impressive, David. Looks like this is going to be second nature to you," Bruce says with a smile.

We leave the basement with Bruce and walk upstairs to check in to the hospital. My parents sign what seem like a million pieces of paper, and then we meet Nurse Simmons.

"Hi, David. I'm Nurse Simmons." She holds out her right hand, and I use my new myoelectric arm to shake her hand. I'm careful not to close it too hard. "Wow, you are already really good with that hand. I'm one of the nurses who will be on your floor. Are you ready to come up and get settled?"

"I guess," I reply.

She leads us to the elevator, and we go to the third floor. We walk down some hallways then enter a big room with a huge desk with several nurses working.

"Hi, everyone. This is David, and he's going to be staying with us for a while as he learns to use his new prosthesis," Nurse Simmons announces.

The other nurses say hello and wave to me as we enter. My parents and I say hi back. The room seems enormous. There is this big desk that makes a circle, and there are six rooms that extend from around the desk.

"You are in Room A," Nurse Simmons says. "Come this way."

She guides us to our room. There are six beds on each side of the wall. Most of them have things on the shelves near the beds. Books, toys, hats, pictures. Things that let you know someone is calling that bed home.

"I'll let y'all get settled in," Nurse Simmons says as she makes her way back to the big desk outside the room.

"How's this bed look, David?" my mom asks.

I nod my head yes, not knowing what else to do. It starts to hit me that I am going to be alone here. My parents help me unpack my suitcase and put my clothes into the drawer next to the bed.

My mom takes out a framed picture of our family we took at our church. "I brought this so you can look at it and remember how much we love you."

I can tell she is starting to cry. I don't want to cry, but the realization that they are leaving me starts to hit me. I hug them both, and we are all teary. Mostly my mom and me. My parents leave, and I am truly alone in the room. I look at this new prosthesis. I practice opening and closing it. I look in the mirror by the bathroom to see how realistic it looks. Will this work? Will this make me normal enough for a girl to want to be my girlfriend?

"Looking good, hotshot, but if you don't mind, I need to get in that bathroom," says a guy in a wheelchair behind me.

"Oh, I'm sorry, dude. I was just practicing using this thing," I reply.

"No worries. I'm Toby, by the way."

"Nice to meet you, Toby. I'm David."

He gives a smile and then kinda nods his head to say, "I gotta use that bathroom." I quickly move out of the way and make my way back to my bed.

I go to my bed and watch as the other guys come into the room for the night. Everyone says hello, and they invite me to watch the television in the game room. The nurses bring us our dinners, and we have ice cream for dessert. As we go back to the bedroom, I notice I am the only one walking on two legs. Some of the guys are using wheelchairs, a few use walkers, and a couple of guys are on crutches as they learn to use prosthetic legs. It's just a passing thought. I notice them like I am sure people notice me. We are different and learning to adapt.

The next day we have "school" at the hospital. The room has desks like a regular school, and the teacher, Mrs. Dickerson, brings me my folder.

"Here are the assignments your teachers sent for you to work on this week, David."

The folder is huge! I go through it, and there are countless worksheets for math, English, and science. So much to read. My science teacher sent fun worksheets about George Washington Carver, who found all kinds of uses for the peanut. I spend most of the time working on that and avoiding the math and English. Soon the day is over, and I have to go to occupational therapy. Ms. Littleton is my therapist. She is pretty young, I think. She has me work on using my new prosthesis to pick up toys and then a Coca-Cola can. I have to be very careful with the can because if I close my prosthesis too tight, I will crush the can.

"So you have to get a feel for not squeezing too tight. You don't want to crush the can and spill Coke all over us," Ms. Littleton says with a smile.

I focus on closing it just tight enough. The first time, I don't quite have a full grip because I'm scared to do it too tight, but by the third time, I'm picking it up and putting it down without a problem.

"Great, David," Ms. Littleton says. "You want to try shaking hands?"

She holds out her right hand, and I carefully open my prosthetic hand. I slowly begin to flex my muscle to close it and get the sense when it is just tight enough. We shake.

"Wow." She smiles. "You have got a great handle on this already. It takes most people at least a couple of days to get to shaking hands." She winks at me. "You keep practicing with the other boys and nurses. I'll see you tomorrow, and we will be tying shoes before you know it."

That afternoon I go out to play basketball. I'm shooting by myself, playing my own game of H-O-R-S-E.

"Mind if I join?"

I look over and see Toby. I'm thinking, "How is he going to play in his wheelchair?"

I think he sees my thoughts on my face and says, "Just pass the ball, dummy."

I pass to him, and he shoots from the foul line. *Swish.* "Wow," I am thinking.

"Wanna play H-O-R-S-E?" I ask.

"Sure. Just no three-pointers, OK?" he replies.

We play a close game of H-O-R-S-E, and I win by one shot. "Good game," Toby says. "We better get back upstairs. It's almost dinnertime."

We head back and get in the elevators. "How do you like that new hand?" Toby asks.

"It's OK," I reply. "It's kinda heavy and bulky, but I'm hoping it looks real enough that maybe I can get a girl to be my girlfriend, you know?"

"Why would you want a girlfriend who only likes you because it looks like you have two hands?"

"I don't know. I just think it would make them more comfortable . . . I don't know."

"Well, I'm not going to have a girlfriend who wants me to walk," Toby says confidently. "I'm going to have one who wants to go ninety miles per hour on a chair ride!"

The elevator door opens. "See you at dinner, lover boy." Toby laughs as he exits.

I step out of the elevator and stand in front of the door for a second. I watch Toby wheel himself confidently into our room for dinner. I think Toby helps me see how others might look at me. I am usually the last one picked if I'm on the basketball court and no one knows me. I would have picked Toby last too before I saw him play. I wish I had his confidence. I go to my bed and put my new prosthetic arm back on. I open and close it, listening to the motor make a slight grinding noise. I know it's not perfect, but this must be it. This must be the tool that gets the girlfriend.

CHAPTER 8

A LUKE SKYWALKER HAND

THE WEEK IS OVER BEFORE I KNOW IT, and my parents come to pick me up. It is so good to see them. I've never been gone from home this long, and I am ready to get back. My mom helps me pack up my stuff, and I say goodbye to the guys in the room.

"Take care of yourself, lover boy." Toby laughs as we start to leave.

"You too, Toby. Have fun with those ninety-mile-per-hour rides," I quip with a wink.

The drive home is long and boring. But we get to stop and stay with Grandma and Pop Pop for a night. I show them my new prosthetic hand, and they are amazed by what I can do. I help Grandma in the kitchen and feel proud of how I'm using this new device.

We get home on a Saturday, and I go out on my bike to show off my new myoelectric hand. It's cool I can hold on to the handlebars of my bike. I don't feel like I'm always leaning forward the way I do when riding with my nub. I ride with my brother Kenneth to the bike trails behind the neighborhood playground.

"Whoa. What is that?" asks Jeremy Brower. He's, like, the oldest kid in our neighborhood.

"It's my new hand," I reply. "Watch this." I open the hand and take it off the handlebars. I proceed to close it and reopen it to *oohs* and *ahhs* from the other kids.

"It's like a Luke Skywalker hand!" says Jason Bronson.

"So cool," says Christie Johnson. "How strong is it?"

"Let me shake your hand," I say.

I might have squeezed a little too hard on purpose.

"Ouch! Whoa, whoa, whoa, let go!" screams Christie.

I release the hand, and she shakes her hand quickly. "That hurt, dude!"

"I'm sorry. I guess I don't know my own strength," I reply. I kinda do, but it was fun to punish Christie a little bit. She is a bit bossy.

"I know what we should do," says Jeremy Brower. "We should play *Star Wars*! David, that is, like, the perfect Luke Skywalker hand. I can be Darth Vader, and we can use the tree house as Cloud City."

"Oh, sweet," says Christie. "I can be Princess Leia, of course, and since it is Cloud City, Jason, you can be Han Solo. We can do the carbonite part—you know, when Princess Leia says, 'I love you' and Han Solo says, 'I know.'"

Jason rolls his eyes.

"What can I be?" says my brother Kenneth. He's so much younger and kinda annoying.

"You can be Yoda," I say.

"Yes, absolutely," replies Jeremy. "Yoda is the coolest of the characters. We need to get you to the Dagobah system. I think that is maybe out in the marsh."

"Yeah, I know just the place," I say. "There is this old log out there, which is the perfect place for Yoda's home."

We wander through the marsh and find the old log in the marsh for Yoda's home.

"Stay here, and we will come visit you after we finish playing in Cloud City. We will do the whole training of Luke Skywalker part," I promise.

We take back off on our bikes and ride to the tree house behind Jeremy's house. We suffer through Christie playing her love scene with Han Solo, but then they both become imperial guards, and Jeremy and I have this epic lightsaber battle. We are on the ropes of the tree house; we climb the trees next to the house. It is so much fun. We have, like, three or four battles because it is so cool to sling my new arm off when Darth Vader strikes it. Christie as Princess Leia rescues me as I hang upside down from the rope ladder leading to the tree house. Jason changes to be Lando Calrissian for this part.

We have a blast. Soon, I hear my mom calling. I know it's time to head home and get ready for dinner. I look at my prosthetic hand. It's a little dirty, because it took a lot of falls during our playtime. I say bye to everyone and get on my bike. I walk into the house and take my arm to my room; I don't want to let my mom see how dirty it is.

"Where's your brother?" my mom asks.

Oh, no. "The Dagobah System!" I yell as I run outside to my bike. I race to the marsh and find Kenneth sitting on the log. "Hey, Yoda," I say.

"Time for training it is," says Kenneth without hesitation.

"Yes. But I think you need to train me on the way home. It's dinnertime."

I don't think Kenneth realizes how much time has passed, but he and I play Yoda training Luke as we wait for dinner and then before bedtime. He's actually a pretty good Yoda. Who knew?

That Monday I go back to school. At first no one really notices my new arm. I cleaned it up pretty well, so it blends in with my skin. Finally, Wyman says, "Hey, Harrell, you have a hand." That brings attention to it. Soon lots of people are looking at it and asking how it works. Cool kids are asking about it. Even some of the girls from the infamous lunch table are curious.

"Your new hand is pretty cool," says Samantha Parker.

"Thanks," I reply. "Let me show you how it works."

I take off my arm and show Samantha the two electric

buttons that open and close the hand.

"You push this one if you want to open it and this one to close it," I say.

Samantha plays with opening and closing the hand. She laughs and makes this amazing giggle sound as the hand moves with her touch.

"Let me try," says Steve Popkin. Samantha looks at me for an OK. I nod my head, and she lets Steve take the arm. He opens and closes it. He then starts to chase some of the girls with it. They run, laughing and having fun.

"Stop chasing and trying to grab the girls, Popkin," says Coach Ferris loudly.

"I'm not grabbing the girls, Coach. It's David Harrell's hand!" Steve says slyly. Everyone is laughing, and Steve brings me back the arm. "Cool, man, really cool," Steve says.

After school Leslie St. Claire comes up to me and hands me an invitation to her birthday party. It's a big deal. I've never been invited to a popular kid's birthday. I think this new hand could be opening the doors to lots of new possibilities.

CHAPTER 9

DANCING LIKE A WALLFLOWER

THE AMERICAN LEGION HALL is over on Saint Simons Island. It is in a secluded area filled with large oak trees and hanging Spanish moss. My dad pulls the car up to the entrance. "You good?" he asks.

"Yeah, I think so," I reply. I am not really good. I am hopelessly nervous, so I stay in the front seat, staring at the hall.

"I am not much of the dancing type, so if you are going to go to the dance, you are going to need to open the door and go inside."

"OK, Dad." I open the door and breathe in the breeze outside. It is warm and soothing.

"I'll be back at nine p.m.," says Dad as he pulls away.

There are few parents outside the front door talking. I don't know them, and they seem to be really engaged in their conversations. I breathe in that breeze again and allow it to move me forward. I pass the chattering parents and step inside. The main lights are off, and there are colored lights spinning as the music plays loud. No one is on the dance floor; people are gathered on either side of the room. Boys are on one side near the punch bowl, and the girls are on the other side near the desserts and the present table. I have a gift for Leslie: earrings my mom helped me pick out from the Belk department store. I think I should drop the gift off quickly and head to the boys' side. That seems like the rule. I put my gift on the table and say, "Happy birthday, Leslie."

She smiles and says, "Ah, thanks, David. Be sure to grab some cookies."

I pass through the girls, trying to smile, but my eyes go straight to the floor. I see their shoes and the bottom of the tablecloth on the cookie table. Whew. I take a napkin and pick one cookie. I balance it on my prosthesis. I don't want to try to balance more than one.

"Just one cookie?" I hear over my shoulder. It's Samantha Parker.

"Yeah. I'm not really hungry."

"Well, you must try one of these. My mom helped me make them. And who doesn't like oatmeal raisin?" She places three more cookies on my napkin.

"Thanks," I say. I do a weird nod thing and back away to seek the safety of the punch bowl and the boys.

When I get to the boys' side of the room, I see guys I know: the regular crew of Wyman, Dean, and Kane, along with the two Hanks, O'Brian and Yackley. We say "what's up" in a variety of fashions, and I start to nibble on the cookies. Samantha's right: the ones she and her mom made are awesome. I find a safe place at the corner of the table to set the remaining cookies so I can get a drink. I pour the punch into a cup and find space to stand near my cookies. I am super self-conscience with the prosthetic arm. It's hard to hold the cookies, and I am scared I will break the paper cup with the punch if I try to hold it. God, I wish I could have two hands right now. The guys are talking about sports and how we wish we could play some football on the dance floor. Someone finds a tennis ball, and we start to throw it around the room. A makeshift game of tennis-football starts. It's all fun until Troy Blankenship throws the tennis ball into the punch bowl on accident. It is very funny but causes the grown-ups to put a stop to the game. We go back to the wall and stand, no one really knowing what to do.

"It Takes Two" by Rob Base and DJ E-Z Rock comes on. I love this song. The guys start dancing in our corner of the wall. The girls have been dancing on their side for a while, but as the song plays, we begin to come together in the middle of the room. It is amazing. We are jumping and rapping. It is great. The next song is "A Groovy Kind Of Love" by Phil Collins. Slow song. The floor clears except for a few "couples" who stay to slow dance.

I make my way back to my cookies. I bite into another oatmeal raisin.

"Hey, Abner," I hear. It's Christopher Lancaster. "Hey, man, can you go ask Samantha Parker if she'd like to dance with me?"

"And ask Leslie if she will dance with me," pipes up Steve Popkin.

"Sure," I reply. I walk across the floor in a daze. I want to ask Samantha to dance, but why would she dance with me? I find the two girls and relay the requests from Christopher and Steve. The girls look at each other and shyly say, "Sure."

I give Chris and Steve a nod, and they move toward the floor. The girls walk to meet them. Samantha looks back to me, but I quickly avert my eyes and grab another of her mom's cookies.

The night ends with the same things happening in circular fashion. There are upbeat songs that bring us together, then slow songs that cause us to go back to our sides of the room. I ask a few other girls to dance with other boys but never with me. I feel that's best. I don't want to get rejected like Troy Blankenship does with Jody Turner. That's terrible. Shawn Randell asks Jody for Troy, and she runs away with her friends saying, "Oh, my god, no!" Ouch. So I play it safe and take no risks.

My dad is there at nine p.m., and we head home. It's low tide, and you can't see the reflection of the moon on the water in the marsh as we cross the bridge to return from Saint Simons Island. I feel like the mud in the marsh. Stuck. My dad asks how things went, and I say fine. I tell him about the tennis ball flying into the punch and how my team had scored a couple of touchdowns before that incident. That's all there is to tell.

School is pretty much the same with my new prosthetic hand. Guys want to play with it and try to squash milk cartons or chase girls with it. After a while I stop wearing it. It's pretty heavy, and it's hard to use it for anything I like doing, like PE or art. No one seems to mind. A few guys ask where it is at first, but soon people just forget about it.

One day in music class we're using our hands to clap out rhythms of notes. With my nub I must place it very specifically in my left hand to make a clap sound. I'm not sure if I'm just nervous or what, but I can't get my nub to make a sound with my hand. Our teacher Ms. DeAngelo tells me to not worry and to use my foot to stomp out the beat. It's embarrassing, and I can feel everyone staring at me as I slam my foot into the carpet, making a muffled thud sound.

As we're leaving the class, Christopher Lancaster puts his right arm inside his sleeve and mocks me: "Hey, y'all, I'm David Harrell, and I only have one hand. I can't make any sounds when I clap. Can I smack you on the book bag to make some noise?" He smacks Tommy Sullivan's book bag, and everyone laughs. I laugh too. I don't know what else to do.

At lunch it gets worse. As I sit at the boys' table, Christopher Lancaster says, "Hey, guys, I'm David Harrell, and I only have one hand." He has his right arm in his sleeve again. "I can't open my milk carton by myself. Could someone open it for me? No, wait, I know. I'll open it with my teeth like a cow. Mooooooooooooo! Mooooooooooooo!" He bites into his milk carton and pretends to open it.

It's true: milk cartons are hard to open one-handed. A lot of days I ask someone to help me open it, usually Mike Kelsey because he's quiet, and I interpret that as nice.

Everybody laughs at Christopher's interpretation of me opening my milk carton with my teeth. That's also true. I can do it, but it's an awkward and ugly process of me ripping and pulling the carton with my mouth. I laugh too. What else is there to do? When those instances happen, I just feel small, and I feel that no one really likes me. No one really accepts me; I'm just entertainment.

I feel like I want to hide. I ask Mr. Eckleheart during the next period if I can go to the bathroom. I take the hall pass and leave. When I get to the bathroom, I start crying. I'm not sure where it comes from; it just flows out. I want to tell Christopher Lancaster to shut up, but it just comes out as tears in the stall. I calm down a little bit and start my way back to class. As I walk down the hall, Ms. Lansford, our guidance counselor, passes me. "Hi, David," she says. The tears come again from nowhere. "What's wrong?" she asks with her arm around my shoulder. I can't speak. I just cry. "Why don't you come with me to my office? I'll let Mr. Eckleheart know."

Ms. Lansford's office is small. Stuffy but comfortable. There are so many posters and pictures on the wall, you almost forget it's a plain cinder block school wall in the room. "What's going on, David? You seem very upset."

I stare at the floor. I can't tell her. If I say these guys are making fun of my hand or laughing at me because I'm different, what will happen? They'll be called to the principal's office. They'll know I tattled. I mean, I laughed too. Do they even know what they are saying hurts me? Does it hurt me? Am I just being a baby?

"I just get mad sometimes," I say to her, continuing my laser focus on the floor.

"Mad at what?" she replies. "Mad at somebody? Mad at yourself? Mad at the world?" she questions.

"I don't know. A little of all of that, I guess," I reply. "Maybe I sometimes think if I could just be like everyone else, if that was the case, then I would fit in."

"So, if you were different, you think you would fit in?" Ms. Lansford asks.

"Yeah, if I had two hands, then I wouldn't be different. I would fit in." Whoa. I just said it. I wish I had two hands. Is that true? I thought I was over it.

"I see," Ms. Lansford says slowly. "Well, I've got some bad news for you, kid. You are not going to have two hands. Your disability is part of who you are. And that is not a bad thing. Think of all the things you do. Your lack of one hand has not held you back." She stares at me, and I bring my eyes from the floor to connect with hers. "Let me let you in on a little secret. I talk to a lot of your classmates, and you are certainly not the only one who doesn't think they fit in. They all have two hands, so I don't think you missing a hand is the problem."

My eyes move back to the floor. My forehead squishes together as I try to process what she just said.

"We all feel that we don't fit in sometimes. That is a very universal feeling. One way to feel better about it is to take action. What is something you could do to make yourself feel like you are moving forward?" she asks, looking for an answer.

"I don't know," I reply. What is this, a test?

"Well, how about this? You take some time and think about it. Come back in a few days and tell me what you come up with. Sound good?"

"Yeah," I say, looking forward to leaving the office.

I walk back to Mr. Eckleheart's class with that question burning in my head. What can I do? What should I do? The rest of the day passes, and I feel better. My thoughts are about what I can do to move forward. Something that takes me away from not liking myself. Something I can control.

After dinner I go to my room and stare at my nub. Is this the problem?

"No, this is not the problem, fool," says Mr. Mo.

"Then what is?" I ask.

"You are scared, fool; you are scared to put your whole self out there."

"Because what if everyone points or everyone laughs?" I retort. "What could I do to really put all of myself out there?" I ask.

"Run for student council" is Mr. Mo's reply.

My heart drops. I've seen the poster in Ms. Lansford's office that said "Student Council Elections Sign-Up." I knew Mr. Mo was right, and I knew deep inside I wanted to do it.

"Ladies love a politician," Mr. Mo says slyly. "It's a way to maybe find that girlfriend you are looking for, fool."

That night at dinner, I say to my mom, "I think I'm going to run for student council."

"That is brilliant!" my mom replies. "I think that is a great idea."

"What's your campaign slogan going to be?" asks my brother Kenneth.

"I don't know," I reply. I haven't thought that far in advance.

"Get ready for Dave the Rave!" my dad says, smiling.

"David Can Rock Better than Your Pet Rocks," says my baby brother Bennett.

"I don't know," I say. "Maybe."

"Catch the Wave, Vote for Dave," my mom says.

We all look at each other. That's it! Catch the Wave, Vote for Dave.

CHAPTER 10

CATCHING THE WAVE

I GO TO SCHOOL THE NEXT DAY feeling really good. I have a bit of a pep to my step. Catch the Wave, Vote for Dave! That sounds great. I go by Ms. Lansford's office. I put my name on the sign-up poster for student council representatives. I give Ms. Lansford a nod as I walk out of the office. I can feel her smiling behind me. I am moving forward, and it feels amazing.

At lunch I come to the table and sit with Wyman, Dean, and Kane. "Guys, I'm running for student council," I say.

"Whoa, that's big," says Wyman. "You sure you want to take that on?"

"You better make snack food in the cafeteria your campaign platform." Dean laughs.

"Yes, we want a candy bar, not a salad bar." Kane laughs as well.

"I'll see what I can do," I say with a laugh of my own.

What do I want to do? I don't have time to think

very much before I hear, "Hey, Abner!" It's Christopher Lancaster. He has his arm buried inside his sleeve. "Hey, guys, I'm David Harrell, and I only have one hand. I can't open my milk carton. Can someone please help me? Ha, ha, ha. Wait. I know. I'll open it with my mouth like a cow! Moooo, mooooo, mooooo!"

Great. Here it is again. The cow bit. Christopher Lancaster starts biting his milk carton and laughing. Everyone starts laughing too. Including me. I kinda shrug my shoulders and bury my milk carton in my mouth. This causes more raucous laughter. Joel Stewart, who is a cool kid but keeps to himself, comes to our table to sit. He looks at the scene of laughter and knows the cow bit is happening. He looks at me. He sees in my eyes that this is painful. My laughing is just covering the pain.

"Dude, that's not cool," he says. And then he walks away to join another table. Everyone at our table stops laughing. Including me. Wyman, Dean, and Kane see me, maybe for the first time. They look at Christopher and then each other. We sit in silence for three to five seconds, looking at each other. Christopher slowly pulls his arm from his sleeve, takes his tray, and walks away. There is this weight on the table, I mean, inside us, I guess. We just sit there staring at our food.

"Sorry, Harrell," Dean says, still looking down at his tray.

"Yeah, sorry, man. That was uncool," Kane replies.

"We should've seen that for what it is," Wyman says.

"I mean, it just seemed like innocent fun."

"I was laughing too," I say. "I guess I just thought if I made you laugh, you would like me. If I made fun of my nub, you would be more comfortable."

"Dude, that sucks you had to feel that way," Wyman says.

"We think you are cool regardless, Harrell. I mean, you are funny even without the nub jokes," Kane replies.

"Well, most of your jokes suck, but we still laugh," Dean says with a smile.

"We are going to have your back now, man. We get it now," says Wyman. He holds his milk carton up. "Cheers."

We raise our cartons in a toast. "Just make sure you get that candy bar for the cafeteria," Dean cracks.

We laugh, and I enjoy lunchtime for the first time in I don't know how long.

When I get home, my mom shows me some picture ideas for posters. I like the one that just has a big blue ocean wave with the words "Catch the Wave, Vote for Dave." My mom uses her Macintosh computer to add pictures and play with the font of the words. They come out great! Even in color. I start to put up the posters throughout the school. Folks are fans of the campaign slogan! Dean starts to move his arms to get people to do the wave in the hallways as I walk by. "Catch the wave, y'all! Vote for Dave!" he says as he walks to class.

Mr. Eckleheart pulls me aside one day after class. "Hey, David, I love how you are running your campaign. Love the slogan. But the facts are, you are running against all the popular kids. They are going to split the vote. You know, three people get to be representatives. So you need to do something to get more people to vote for you. You need to focus on the universal vote. And what is more universal than rap?"

I look at him like he is speaking another language.

"You should rap your speech," he says.

I still can't find words to say. Rap my speech? What does that mean?

"Oh, that would be tight," says Damon Miller. "Nobody would expect that from you, and it would sure be different."

Yeah, it would be different. But I don't want to be different. I want to fit in. I want to be a part of something. I tell my mom what Mr. Eckleheart said when I get home.

"That is brilliant!" she exclaims.

"Oh, no" is my thought.

"She's right," Mr. Mo says when I get to my room.

"How can she be right?" I question. "I'd look stupid. Everybody might laugh at me. What if that happens? People aren't making fun of me right now. If I do something like this, they might start again."

"Sometimes you have to take a risk, fool. Sometimes you step into the unknown. You need to rap this speech."

The next morning my mom slaps down a piece of

paper in front of my cereal. My mom has written a rap for me.

"What do you think?" she asks.

I look it over. I think it looks good. Maybe this will work. After school that day, my mom shows me some changes she's made to the rap. It's even better! We work on making more posters. My brothers even help. We use markers on poster board to make really big signs. It is awesome. We laugh and kid each other. It is a great night.

CHAPTER 11

WHEN YOUR HEART STOPS

WE DON'T QUITE FINISH THE POSTERS before bed, so I jump up early the next morning to finish them. As I am coloring in the enormous wave on the poster board, my dad comes in from the kitchen. I can tell something is wrong.

"You don't have to finish that today, bud," my dad says, his voice cracking a little bit. "Your Pop Pop died this morning."

My heart stops. I feel this weight hit my chest. I stare at my dad, unable to even blink.

"His heart stopped in the middle of the night. They rushed him to the hospital. Your mom left when your grandmother called. He died in the hospital a few hours ago. I'm sorry, bud."

I leave the Magic Marker open and run toward my father. I embrace him with a force that causes him to have to catch his balance. I cry. Hard. He just holds me tight. The world stops for a moment. It feels surreal, as though I am seeing myself from above. It's like a movie. I don't want to feel this feeling. Slowly I find my way back to myself. I move my face away from my dad's now wet shoulder.

"I've got to go wake your brothers up. I need you to be strong with me for them," he says.

I go to the kitchen to make my breakfast. I pour cereal for my brothers and get them milk. We sit in silence and eat. My dad tells us that we are going to get some nice clothes for the funeral and not go to school. We will leave for my grandparents' house after we finish picking out the new clothes. We should get our Sunday school shoes and a nice shirt, my dad tells us as he begins to clean up our cereal bowls.

We arrive at Peter's Men's Shop. My dad's buddy James works there. His dad was the original Pete. James is usually jovial, and he and my dad trade insults most of the time we come in, but not today.

"Sorry to hear about your granddad, boys," James says as we come inside. "Let's get you all some suits that will make him proud as he looks down on you from heaven."

We all take turns trying on black and gray suits. I choose a gray one with pinstripes. I also choose a navy tie. I feel gray like this suit. I have never known anyone who's died. I guess maybe that is wrong. Old people from our church have died, but I didn't really know them. Pop Pop was mine. It's not fair he is gone.

We arrive in my grandparents' town and go straight to the funeral home. There he is, lying in his casket. I can just see the tip of his nose, but I know it is him.

"You don't have to go over if you don't want to," my dad says. My brothers hold on to him, and he leads them toward the back of the funeral home. I see my grandmother sitting near the casket. My mom and her sisters are standing next to her. There is a line of people moving forward to meet them.

I make my way toward my mom. I hug her from the side. She looks at me with her red eyes full of tears and pulls me closer. She fixes my hair a little bit and tries to smile. "I love you," she whispers. I move to hug my aunts and my grandmother. My grandmother looks so frail. I don't mean to, but I instinctively look over to the casket. I see Pop Pop. He looks relaxed but not real. It's like one of those wax figures at Ripley's Believe It or Not! A mannequin. His eyes are closed, and it seems like he's sleeping.

We finish the night by going to my aunt Ruth's house. It is wild being there in this sadness. Every time I've been here, it's been a house of joy. Playing with my cousins' toys or playing football outside. Singing at night with Pop Pop and Grandma. Listening to my mom sing. But now it's just silence and crying. Then there are stories. That brings some laughter. Stories of Pop Pop. His story. I tell everyone how much I loved going to his old house when we were in Kentucky for the reunion. Playing baseball with him. I start to feel all the emotion come out. I can't quite finish the story.

"It's OK, sweetheart," says my grandmother, pulling me in for a hug. "It's all right. He loved you so much. He loved all of us so much."

After dinner, as we are getting ready for bed, my grandmother calls me over. "I wanted to tell you something," she starts. "Pop Pop and I have been praying for you since before you were born. Do you know that?"

"Yes, ma'am," I say sweetly.

"When you were born, we knew you were special. The way you are, you are a gift. You were made the way you are for a purpose. God put you here for something very special. Pop Pop knew you were going to do great things. And I know that too. I love you. Good night." She kisses my cheek.

"Good night, Grandma," I say in return. "I love you."

As I lie in the pullout couch that night trying to sleep, I keep thinking about what Grandma said. I am special. What great things am I here to do? How am I going to do anything special? How am I going to be like those guys after the baseball or football games with their letterman jackets? What girl is going to want to go with someone who looks like me? Maybe if I can get those things, maybe then I'll be special.

As those thoughts race through my head, I start to see myself playing baseball for my high school. Hitting a line drive to right field and stretching it into a double. A headfirst Pete Rose sliding into second base. The dust flying up into the air. The dust starts to grow. It gets larger and larger; it becomes fog. I stand on second base and use my arms to brush away the fog. It begins to clear. It's no longer Edo Miller Park, the high school baseball field; it's a new field. There is something familiar about the field. Where am I? I look down and see I am in another uniform. It's gray, and my pants are baggy. I see other kids on the field, and there is a potato on my jersey. Am I . . . ?

Smack! I'm interrupted by the crack of a wooden bat hitting a ball. I see the ball fly past me as it goes toward left field.

"Run!" I hear a chorus of boys yell. I take off, rounding third and heading home. I see the catcher preparing to catch the ball. I know I must slide. It's a headfirst slide, of course, and my left hand slides across home plate before the catcher can place the tag.

I am swarmed by who I assume are my teammates. They pull me up as we hug and jump for joy. I look at the kid running from the field to join us, the kid who must have hit the ball. It's Pop Pop; I would know him anywhere. He joins us celebrating. We are jumping up and down, and the dust begins to grow. Again, the dust turns to fog. I search for Pop Pop, but it's just fog. I keep walking through the fog. It starts to clear as I hear the creaking of an old wooden floor under my feet. I see that same kid version of Pop Pop in front of me. He is standing in front of a casket. A woman comes and leads him away by his hand; it's his father. The fog comes again. I feel it moving me now. It clears as I see the kid version of Pop Pop scrubbing the wooden floors. Quickly the image changes to him now carrying buckets of water to the kitchen. We move through his house; there are many people at the dinner table. He is serving them food. I see "Boarding House" on top of the window seal. The fog comes again, but it seems to swirl this time. I feel like I am spinning. As it clears, I am in what seems to be a hospital. I see a man lying in bed. A woman comes through the door. It's my grandmother. She is young and beautiful. Glamorous.

"Harold," she says sweetly. Pop Pop turns away. "Don't turn away from me, Harold. I am here."

"Leave me, Catherine," the man replies. "You don't deserve this; you can't wait for me."

"I will always wait for you, Harold. I love you," the woman says.

The fog swells and pulls me upward. I see the young versions of my grandparents at their wedding. They are laughing and dancing. The momentum of the fog spins me again. I see them with their children: my aunts and my mom. Singing at the piano. Laughing, loving, and joyful. The fog lifts around me again as it moves me to a seat. It feels like a wooden bench. I place my hand to feel the wood. My feet seem to be on a bench too. I feel a slight breeze on my face. The fog clears to reveal the bleachers at that same ball field in Kentucky. This time it is old and run-down, as it was when I saw it last summer.

"Pretty good life, wouldn't you say?" a voice says

behind me. It's Pop Pop. I rush up the bleachers to join him.

"Is this a dream?" I ask.

"Yes," he replies.

"I miss you so much, Pop Pop."

"I know," he replies.

"You lost your dad when you were a kid?" I ask. He nods. "You had to go to work as a kid, and why did you get so sick?"

"Well, I had to help my mother. We had a boarding house so we could make enough money to survive. We couldn't afford to hire anyone, so I did the work. As far as being sick, I had tuberculosis. It is a pretty terrible disease. Your grandmother would come and see me every day. I didn't think I would make it, so I would tell her to leave and find someone else. She never did. Maybe that is why I got better. I wanted to make a life with her. We did make a life, a wonderful life. It wasn't easy, and it was full of challenges and disappointments, but we never let that get us down."

"I can understand disappointments," I reply. "I want you to come back."

"Life is full of disappointments, but it's how we handle them that matters. I can't come back, but I'm always here in your memory," he says. "We don't always get what we want, bucko."

"Like I'm never going to have two hands," I say.

"True," he replies. He smiles and pats me on the knee.

"Remember the story I told you about my Little League baseball team? The Little Potatoes and Hard to Peel?"

I nod yes.

"Well, that was just a metaphor for life. We are all playing this game called life, and sometimes we win and sometimes we lose, but no matter what circumstances we find ourselves in, we can never let that peel away the core of who we are." He picks up my nub in his hand. "This." He looks me the eyes deeply. "This is just one of the many differences that make you completely and beautifully *you.*"

The fog swells around his hand and my nub. It engulfs me again, and I wake up on the pullout couch at my cousins' house. It takes a moment for me to process what's just happened. I touch my face and my feel my nub. I am back, and that was a dream. I hold my nub in my left hand. I'm not sure I believe Pop Pop. I mean, it was just a dream.

CHAPTER 12

HOT DOG IS BACK

WE PACK UP THE CARS and begin our journey home. I worry about my mom. I know she is really sad, but I am scared this will change her. What if she starts smoking cigarettes and becomes one of those people who just wear bedroom slippers all day?

Those fears are put to rest in the weeks after we return. Things go back to a new normal. There is sadness, but my mom is really focused on my student council campaign. She makes so many posters and makes my brothers help me put them all around the campus after school. One day she comes excitedly into my room. "David, look at these!" She opens a rectangular box and pulls out pencils with "Catch the Wave, Vote for Dave" ingrained in them. "I saw these, and I thought they were just perfect," she exclaims.

"They look great, Mom!" I reply. They really are cool, and who couldn't use a new pencil?

"I also had the idea of tying ribbons around lollipops that say 'Catch the Wave, Vote for Dave' for you to hand out to your constituents."

My mom may be going a little too far with this campaign thing. Constituents? Who uses words like that?

"Um, Mom, the lollipops may be a little too much," I say. "I think the pencils are great, but bringing candy to school might seem like I'm kind of bribing people."

My mom does the thing where her eyes go up and to the side while she's thinking. "You're right," she says. "Let's just go with the pencils. I don't want some heifer complaining that my boy is bribing anyone." She turns and heads back to the dining room to work on more posters. I pick up my baseball glove and head out the front door.

I am lucky my mom is so fixated on making my student council posters. It gives me time to practice for the upcoming baseball season. It is a big year. I am going to try to play with the glove on my left hand and spin it around Mr. Mo so I can throw the ball with my left hand too.

There is a space between the windows of my bedroom and my brother's bedroom in front of the house that is just brick. I throw the ball against the wall and practice putting the glove on and taking it back off. It is also good for practicing making accurate throws too. If I don't throw the ball straight, it'll go through one of the windows. That'll be bad.

My dad drives up the driveway and watches me play catch. "You sure that is a good idea, David?"

"What? I need to practice."

"Right, but the last thing I need is to have to replace

a window right now. Let me grab my glove, and we can throw."

He heads inside and is back in minutes. I turn and face him. He and I begin to play catch.

"You are getting better," he says.

"Thanks." I smile. I know he is right. I can feel myself getting more comfortable.

Suddenly, he throws a ground ball to my right. I scramble to backhand it and make a turn back across my body to throw the ball.

"Good," he says. He throws a ground ball to my left. I motor in that direction to field the ball. I spin the glove, take the ball, and throw a strike back to him.

My dad nods and starts to throw me pop flies. I can see him smiling as we play catch until dusk. He knows I can do it, and I know he is proud.

The baseball season starts, and my friends are impressed with how I am playing. Coach Bullock says, "Holy cow, Hot Dog! I thought you were Grade A before, but now you are even better than that!"

I am playing with more confidence. I can even hit the ball better without my prosthesis. I balance the bat on my nub and hold it with my left hand. Coach Bullock and my dad try to get me to hit left-handed, but hitting from the right is more natural to me. I hit several hard line drives to left field at practice.

"Well, you keep hitting like that, Hot Dog, and you can bat any way you want," Coach Bullock says with a smile.

I spend so much time practicing baseball and helping my mom put up the posters for student council that I forget to do one important detail: my homework. When the progress reports come out, my grades are not good. I have a D in language arts and in math.

"We are going to have to take a break from baseball," my mom says at dinner, holding my progress report in her hand.

"No, wait! Baseball is the most important thing in my life," I respond.

"Baseball is important, son, but not as important as your grades," my dad says in his serious voice. "You must get your grades up. They will determine your future. Baseball will have to wait."

"What does that mean?" I ask nervously.

"Baseball is over for at least two weeks. You need to get those grades moving up, and then we will see if you can go back to playing baseball," my mom says firmly.

Two weeks? That is four practices and two games! The first two games of the season. I sit and stare at my meat loaf, mashed potatoes, and green beans. "How am I going to get my grades up in two weeks?" I ask.

"Talk to your teachers and see if there is anything you can do for extra credit. You never know until you ask," my dad responds.

The next day I go to see my language arts teacher, Mrs. Jacobs, and my math teacher, Mr. Schneider. They both are nice and listen to me. They are happy I am trying to improve my grades. Both say it is the missing homework that is the biggest problem. I promise to do my homework, and they both give me extra work to help make up for the things I didn't do earlier. That means lots of extra math worksheets for Mr. Schneider and a three-page paper on something I have learned this year for Mrs. Jacobs.

It's hard to miss my baseball practices, but I put so much effort into getting the work done for school. I stay after school in the library to work. It is easier to focus there than at my house with my brothers running around. The math worksheets are easy, but the three-page paper is hard. What have I learned? I think about Pop Pop. I think about him dying and the sadness that I feel. I think about my dream and how he told me that my missing arm is just one of the many things that make me, well, me. I think about how I taught myself to play baseball. It all begins to flow. The pages are done before I know it.

After two weeks my mom talks to my teachers, and they confirm that I am doing better and my grades are improving. She makes me promise I will keep doing my homework.

"Yes!" I say.

"OK, then you can go back to baseball practice today," she responds.

I sprint from the car to get back to the field for practice that afternoon. My friends Geoff Vance, Hank Yackley, and Chad Bullock give me high fives and hugs. They jump around me, saying, "He got the grades; he got the grades!"

Coach Bullock welcomes me back, and I get to work. I play left field, and it is great. My batting improves, and soon we are playing the season. It goes well. Our team is really good, and we win pretty much every game. I feel like I am on top of the world.

CHAPTER 13

THE RAP HEARD ROUND THE WORLD

THE STUDENT COUNCIL ELECTIONS ARE HERE, and I am starting to rethink the whole "rapping in front of the school" idea. My mom has reworked the rap, and we practice it over breakfast, but I am really scared. What if that bullying starts all over again?

"You need to put on your big boy pants and just do it," Mr. Mo tells me on the way to school.

"But what if everybody laughs? What if I fail?" I ask.

"Big boy pants!" is his only reply.

In homeroom Mr. Eckleheart gives me a wink. He tells the class to watch him during my speech, that he is going to give them a "clue" and my speech is going to be something to behold.

After lunch the entire sixth grade gathers in the cafeteria. They have opened the curtain on the stage and set out a podium in the center. The tables are all put away, and there are just rows of chairs as far as the eye can see. The other candidates sit with me in chairs on the stage. Each of us gets ready to give our speech. My heart is beating so fast, and my palms are wet like I've been swimming in the ocean. This is such a bad idea. Everyone else is just going to talk and read the words they have written on the page. Wait a minute. What if I just read the words my mom created? That is safer. I don't have to rap. I can just read it, and it won't seem too different.

Brandy Roundtree goes first. She is running unopposed for president. Then come the others running for officers: vice president, secretary, and treasurer. Finally, it is the folks running for representative. The student body gets to pick three of us to be on the council.

As it is getting close to my turn, I see my mom come in the side door of the cafeteria. She has my brother Bennett by the hand and walks to the back of the room. She is smiling so big. She is proud of me. I walk to the podium and look out on the entire sixth grade. Mr. Eckleheart gives me a nod, and Jody Thompson from my homeroom says, "Oh, my good lord."

I take a deep breath; I close my eyes and step into the unknown . . .

"My name is Dave, but they call me the Rave,
And I'm here to ask you to catch the wave . . ."

Mr. Eckleheart lifts his hands and starts to clap. My homeroom joins him. Slowly the other students and teachers join.

"Leadership and responsibility,
Yo, they both mean so much to me.
So give me a chance to exhibit these
By electing me as your representative, boy!"

Now the entire cafeteria is clapping and stomping to the beat.

"Tomorrow is the day that you cast your vote,
So grab your board and don't ride the boat.
Vote for David Harrell and you vote for me,
And we'll ride that wave to Glynn Academy.

Peace," I say as I cross my arms and channel my best chill pose.

There is a moment of silence as the clapping ends. Then an eruption of applause and then a standing ovation. I've never received a standing ovation before. I feel like I am floating. I see my mom clapping and crying at the same time. Bennett is jumping in the air and cheering. I float back to my seat, and Tonya Atwater, who is going next, whispers, "I don't like you."

"I guess not *all* girls like politicians," I whisper to Mr. Mo.

"No, but this moment is pretty cool, man. This moment is pretty cool," he replies.

He is right. This is pretty cool.

The next day is the election. I am nervous. I bring

more of the pencils with "Catch the Wave, Vote for Dave" inscribed in them. My mom tied red, white, and blue ribbons around them to make them look extra special. I get a lot of high fives throughout the day. Walking through the hallway, I hear a familiar voice yell, "Hey, Abner!" I see Christopher Landcaster hanging out of Ms. Strickland's doorway. "I'm going to catch the wave, dude! That speech was awesome!"

The list of election winners is posted on a poster board near the cafeteria. There is a big group of people around it as I slowly walk toward it. As people begin to walk away, I notice a few smiling at me. Could I have done this? I get to the poster board and see the names. My name is there. I am one of the three representatives. I blink my eyes a couple of times and look again to make sure. It is still there.

"Congratulations, David," I hear behind me. I turn around and see Ms. Lansford. She is smiling.

"Thanks," I reply.

"That speech of yours was a big hit. I think you showed a lot by doing something different and fun."

"I guess," I say as I shrug my shoulders.

"Let me let you in on a little secret," Ms. Lansford says as she guides me away from the crowd at the poster board. "Every student in the sixth grade voted for you as one of their three choices for representative. Some might have done that because you had a fun speech, but most of them did because you are good person. They see someone who doesn't let difficult things get them down."

"But I do let difficult things get me down sometimes," I reply.

"We all do, kid," she says sweetly. "And maybe your difficult things are more visible, but the fact is we all have them. They see you moving through challenges, and when you get in front of them without fear and entertain them . . . well, they are impressed. Just like I've always been." She winks, pats my shoulder, and leaves me with the masses in the hallway.

I turn to walk back to my class and almost run right into Gretchen Pruitt.

"Oh, my gosh, David," she says.

"Sorry, I just wasn't watching where I was going," I say. Gretchen is one of the super popular girls who didn't win in the election.

"No worries," she says. "I really liked your speech yesterday. That took a lot of courage. I could never do that. I almost threw up before I walked up on that stage. I think you are going to be awesome on student council," she says with a smile. She motions for me to come closer and whispers, "I totally voted for you. See you around later."

CHAPTER 14

HARD TO PEEL

THE REST OF THE SPRING GOES AMAZING. School is fun and baseball is even better. Our team is so good! I also get to pitch more this year. My dad suggested it to Coach Bullock. I mean, Jim Abbott is doing awesome as a pitcher, so maybe I could too. I do a good job pitching. It is a lot of pressure, but I am starting to like it.

"You don't have to strike everybody out, Hot Dog," Coach Bullock tells me at practice. "You have a great defense behind you; just throw strikes and let the other boys take care of the rest."

This is good advice. I don't have to be perfect and have a million strikeouts. I just have to do my best and throw strikes. My friends have my back and will make outs for me. But if I'm honest, it does feel amazing to strike someone out. I just don't have to rely only on myself; we're a team.

The end of the season comes, and we're in the championship game. Big deal. We play well. Our best pitcher, Trevor Wainwright, is pitching. I get a base hit and score a run. We are winning five to two in the bottom of the last inning. Trevor is getting tired but still pitching well. He walks a batter to start the inning, which is never a good start. I'm in left field and cheering him on. He's got this. The next batter pops a foul ball over the third base line. I run as fast as I can but see our third baseman, Brad Campbell, has it with no problem. One out. "We have got this," I say as I smack my nub into my glove.

The next batter hits a deep fly ball to left center field. "Crap!" I say loudly as I run back toward the ball. Can I get there to catch it? I see our center fielder, Chad Bullock, running too. We both realize that we are not going to catch this one, and it soars over the fence. The other team and their fans go nuts. It's now five to four with only one out. Alex Andrews, our catcher, goes out to the mound to settle down Trey. I know he is super mad. Chris, our right fielder Hank O'Brian, and I meet in center field. We don't say much. We all have concern on our faces. We are so close to winning.

"We are going to win this game," Hank O'Brian says. "I don't know how, but we are going to win."

"Just two more outs," I say.

We go back to our positions once Alex Andrews starts back to home plate.

"You got this, Trevor!" we say. "Just two outs!"

Trevor walks the next batter on four straight pitches. Crap. My head drops into my glove. Coach Bullock comes out of the dugout. I think Trevor is just tired. He has pitched so well the entire game. Coach Bullock motions to left field and waves me in. "Let's go, Hot Dog!"

My stomach drops. I look over to Chad and Hank in the outfield. They nod and clap with their gloves. I start running toward the pitching mound. My heart is beating out of my chest. I get to Coach and Alex Andrews at the pitcher's mound.

"All right, Hot Dog, I need you to be Grade A right now." Coach Bullock laughs. "We need two outs. Remember, you don't have to strike everybody out. Throw strikes and believe in your team behind you."

"Let's go, Harrell. You got this," Alex Andrews says as he pats my back with his catcher's mitt, the dust flowing from my back and disappearing in the air.

"I've got this," I say to myself as I throw warm-up pitches to Alex. My arm feels good. I throw until the umpire says, "Last one."

I catch the ball, and the sound hits me like a wave: the cheers from the other team and their fans, the well-wishes from my team and our fans. I wasn't thinking about any of that before this moment. I stand on the mound with both feet and prepare for my windup.

"*Stretch!*" I hear in a voice above all the other noise. It is my dad. Right. There is a runner on first. If I wind up, he can easily steal second.

"*Think!*" my dad yells above the noise and uses both hands to point to his head.

Yes, think. There is a runner on first, so I slowly take

a step off the mound. I walk backward to not indicate I am starting the windup toward home plate. I take a deep breath. I pick up the rosin bag and give myself a chance for another deep breath. "I got this," I whisper to myself. I go back to the mound in the stretch so I can keep an eye on the runner at first. I get set and throw the ball as hard as I can to home plate. It is *way* outside! Alex makes an amazing catch to save the ball from going to the backstop. "I don't got this," I think to myself.

Alex presses his hands toward the ground, a symbol to calm down. He throws the ball back to me, and the noise seems to escalate. My heart is beating so fast, and it feels like the ball field is spinning. I turn away from home plate and see my teammates behind me. Brad Pressler at third, Jimmy Armit at short, Geoff Vance at second, Trevor Wainwright at first. I am not alone. Whatever the outcome of this may be, we are in this together. There is comfort in that. I don't have to do this alone. The noise seems to turn into a hum. I can feel my breath. I see Coach Bullock in my mind saying, "Just throw strikes and trust your teammates." He is right. I focus on the mound again. I check the runner at first. Just throw a strike and get a ground ball. I start my throw, and I swear things start to move in slow motion.

I watch the ball moving to the plate. I see the batter's eyes light up. He swings. *Clank.* It's a ground ball to third. Brad Pressler scoops it up and throws to Geoff Vance, who turns the double play. When Trevor catches the ball at first and the final out is made, I throw my glove into the air. I jump into Alex Andrews's arms, and we are bombarded on the pitcher's mound! After we celebrate, we line up and shake hands with the other team. We then run to the dugout, jumping and hugging each other. "That's a way to be Grade A, Hot Dog!" Coach Bullock says as he gives me a big hug. I run to hug my dad and mom. This is soaring!

The next week is the All-Star tryouts, and I play well. I'm nervous but confident my name will be on the list this year. I run once the list is up to look. There is my name: David Harrell. I start to cry. I'm not sure why, but it just comes out of nowhere. I walk quickly away and find a safe corner in the rec building where no one can see me. "It's OK to be proud," Mr. Mo says softly. I nod my head and breathe. The tears slow down, and I allow myself to feel good.

As I head out of the building, I see Coach Bullock. "I am proud of you, Hot Dog. You really worked hard, and you've had a great season. There's somebody I want you to meet."

"Hey, David. I'm Coach Bryant from Glynn Academy," says the man.

"I know, Coach. I've seen you at the games since I was little," I reply.

"Yeah, I've seen you around since you were little. Congratulations on the All-Star team. Look forward to seeing you soon at Glynn Academy." He gives me a fist bump. "Keep up the good work."

Amazing! The high school coach knows me and is looking forward to me being there. "You are on your way to that letterman jacket, fool!" says Mr. Mo as we walk to my dad's car.

"I think you're right, Mr. Mo," I whisper silently. My dad looks at me as I approach the car. I give him a smile and thumbs-up. He knows I made it. He hits the steering wheel of the car, smiles, and nods. I get in, and we ride home talking about baseball.

I'd be lying if I said I wasn't counting down the days until the summer, but I don't mind going to school each day. I think I learn more too, actually. Lunch is fun, no milk carton jokes, just laughs and high fives throughout the day. In one of the final nights before the end of school, we have our school dance. This dance is a little better than Leslie's birthday party. It's at the school, which makes it more comfortable, and there are hardly any slow songs. We all dance to the fast songs and have so much fun. It really is a great night. I am definitely soaring! There is a pickup football game in the quad. The boys and girls play, which is fun and hilarious. The girls are pretty good too, and it's cool having them have fun with us.

The night is winding down, and I am with several guys getting the last of the sodas to cool down from our football game and dancing. The music changes, and it's a slow song. A few guys who are going with girls rush away to slow dance. I sigh and sip my root beer.

"Hey, Abner," I hear from Christopher Lancaster behind me. "Will you go ask Samantha Parker if she will dance with me?"

It is amazing how fast you can go from soaring to landing flat and all the air in your stomach escaping from a gut punch. "Sure," I respond. I don't know why I agree, but it just seems like the right thing to do. I walk across the gym floor to where Samantha is talking to her friends.

"Hey, Samantha," I say quietly.

"Yeah?" she replies.

"Um . . . would you like to dance with . . . me?"

I don't know where it comes from; it just comes out of my mouth. I forget all about Christopher Lancaster; I just see her.

"Absolutely," she says and takes my left hand in hers. We walk to the middle of the gym. She wraps her arms around my neck, and my arms slide around her waist. I see Christopher Lancaster out of the corner of my eye; he is staring with his mouth wide open. Bobby Adams and Justin Purvis give an audible "Ha!" to him and walk away laughing. Christopher laughs to himself and nods. I think he realizes he should have the courage to ask himself. We are all still learning, I guess.

The song, "A Groovy Kind Of Love" by Phil Collins, plays as Samantha and I sway together slowly. Her curly black hair tickles my cheek a little bit. I smell her perfume again. The best way to describe it is a tingle. My shoulders and my neck are tingling, and the rest of my body seems to be floating. We are both floating. I don't want this song to end, but it does. I smile at Samantha, and she smiles back. We don't say anything, which is weird. I don't know if we know what to say. I go back over to the sodas, and she returns to her friends.

The dance ends, and I walk out with my friends. I see my dad's car parked down the street. I realize for the first time something is ending. I survived sixth grade, but maybe I survived something more. Life as I knew it will not be the same. There is a little sadness in that feeling. I walk off toward my dad's car alone.

"David," I hear behind me. It's Samantha Parker. She runs up to me and hands me a piece of notebook paper folded up. She kisses me on the cheek and runs back in the other direction.

"David, let's go," I hear my dad say from his car. I pick up the pace and pass by the giant oak trees. I get into the passenger seat. "You have a good time?" my dad asks.

"Yes, sir, I had a great time," I answer quickly. I look back at the school as we drive away.

I feel the paper folded up in my left hand. I open it and see "Samantha 264-0508" with a heart exclamation point at the end. My eyes widen, and my breath draws up in surprise.

"You did it, fool," Mr. Mo says from his reflection in

the window. "You might get a girlfriend, and you are on your way to getting the letterman jacket. It's what you've always wanted, right?"

"I don't know, Mr. Mo," I say silently in my heart. "What happens if I get those things and it ends up not being what I want?"

"You keep moving forward, fool" is his reply.

"Right." I laugh to myself.

I look out the passenger window as we cross over the giant Sidney Lanier Bridge. You can see the pathway to the ocean from here. The reflection of the full moon shines on the waves of water leading to the horizon, the vastness of what lies ahead. It is like I am flying; I am above everything and heading somewhere new. I don't know what is coming next, but I am excited. I think of Pop Pop up in the stars.

"I don't know why I was born into this world like I am," I say silently to Mr. Mo. "But I do know that right here, right now, I am here and playing this game of life as hard as I can . . . and I am going to be hard to peel."

I look back at Samantha's phone number in my hand, and I see Mr. Mo's reflection in the moonlight. He smiles, and I smile back.

THE REAL DAVID

Epilogue

The real David is not far from the David you just read about in my book. All the stories that make up this story come from a place of truth. I did accomplish things I wanted to do as a kid. I earned letterman jackets in football and baseball at my high school. Girlfriends came into my life as well. I accomplished the "things" I wanted but it didn't seem to be enough. The outside accomplishments would never make me feel normal. I had to learn the lessons of this book: that my missing right hand is just one of the many differences that make me beautifully and wonderfully "me."

So why the funny title? Well, it is a true story. Pop Pop told all his grandchildren the story. He told it because it is universal. Life is hard. Not just now, but it always has been. In fact, it's not supposed to be easy. We grow from adversity. All of us will face challenges, difficult circumstances, or have limitations placed on us in one form or another. Our choice is to not allow those things to peel away our humanity, our toughness. Our journey through life will have many ups and downs, twists and turns, but what I want you to remember from this book are that your differences make you beautiful and unique.

You have an amazing journey ahead of you. Find goals and dreams of what you want to do and set forth. And, when the hardships come—and they will—remember my story.

Actually, you know what? Remember my granddad's story. Pop Pop. Remember that you too can be *A Little Potato and Hard to Peel.*

About the Author

DAVID HARRELL is an actor, writer, speaker, and disability advocate. In 2021, he was honored by the Casting Society of America as one of the Top 20 Actors from underrepresented populations. Television credits include *The Gilded Age, FBI: Most Wanted, The Code, Bull*, and *Law & Order: Special Victims Unit*. On stage, he has performed Off-Broadway and regionally across the country. His award-winning solo plays *A Little Potato and Hard to Peel* and *The Boy Who Would Be Captain Hook* continue to entertain audiences of all ages. He received the Distinguished Service Award from the New Jersey Governor's Awards for Arts in Education in 2019. He was nominated in 2010 for a New York Innovative Theatre Award for Outstanding Solo Performance and won the 2014 Journalist Choice Award for his work in a solo play festival in Pärnu, Estonia. He currently lives in Savannah, Georgia with his family.